WHEN AUTUMN FALLS

Maria Holder

MINERVA PRESS
LONDON LEICESTER DELHI

WHEN AUTUMN FALLS
Copyright © Maria Holder 2002

All Rights Reserved

No part of this book may be reproduced in any form
by photocopying or by any electronic or mechanical means,
including information storage or retrieval systems,
without permission in writing from both the copyright
owner and the publisher of this book.

ISBN 0 75411 699 9

First Published 2002 by
MINERVA PRESS
St Georges House
6 St Georges Way
Leicester LE1 1SH

WHEN AUTUMN FALLS

This book is dedicated to all those who believed in me...

Chapter One

It was late autumn, and the leaves were just turning to that beautiful bronze colour which gave the park a beautiful warm glow in the sunlight. Stephanie loved the autumn, Jack always seemed to be asleep in his pram when she took them to the local park. Callum was just building up the kind of confidence to run and laugh with the freedom of the great outdoors. He had gorgeous thick blonde curly hair and big blue eyes. A gust of wind almost blew Callum off his feet, as he rushed through the pile of golden leaves that had mounted under the huge old trees.

He went everywhere in his green wellingtons with frog eyes on the front of his feet. He had seen them the month before, on a shopping trip, and pleaded for a pair. His father Richard had taken them all for a day out shopping, which was Jack's first major outing since being born. Stephanie didn't feel the weather would be very nice so they all jumped into the family car, and drove to Stephanie's favourite shopping complex. And it was there Callum had spotted these cute Wellingtons. After all it was a family thing, and on these kind of trips it was usually the children who got what they needed first.

But little did Stephanie know that just one incident on this special family outing would blow their world apart.

They had always had a perfect relationship, married at a sensible time in their lives. Richard and Stephanie had known each other for several years during university, he had studied law and Stephanie thrived from her studies as a fashion student. Somehow they hadn't really noticed each other in a romantic sense, until their paths had crossed at a friend's dinner party, with some more than elegant, charming friends. It was at the party that they became locked in conversation. And, as they say, some people are made for each other. Richard was fair-haired and so handsome. They hung on every word they said to one another. It was as though their friends knew they were perfect for each other, and they weren't wrong. The dinner party had gone to the extreme of perfection and certain friends of Stephanie were more than pleased with themselves. And at times Stephanie and Richard would reminisce about how they first met and never looked back.

On that day, in the centre of one of Stephanie's favourite exclusive stores, she noticed a young couple of teenage lovers and pointed them out to Richard, who giggled to himself with memories of his own. They both remembered how it was when they walked arm in arm and were constantly kissing in public. They still did from time to time, but Stephanie was long since a teenager, and Richard was just a little older than she was.

It seemed important to go places as a proper family, and enjoy time together, as Richard well respected. Time with his family was very special to him. His sons meant the world to him, as did Stephanie, his wife. But something seemed to distract him from time to time, though Stephanie hadn't noticed as Richard kept it to himself. She had never known anything other than her perfect life, and her perfect family. Everything had happened so naturally, first university and gradually getting what she wanted in life, then Richard. They were so in love and happy. Her career had taken off modestly and slowly. She built herself up and her knowledge of fashion had taken her to the height she wanted to achieve. Stephanie socialised very little to begin with, but as her relationship became more personal they went out more often with friends and clients from which the law firm Richard belonged to.

Life was indeed busy and very much what she had longed for. As they left the store they realised they had to go for lunch. Jack was due for a bottle-feed soon and Callum was getting a little irritable as he was hungry. Stephanie and Richard found an ideal restaurant and they were seated immediately. Callum wasn't a fussy child with his food but today he seemed a little irritable at the table. And to the untrained eye the reason for the boy's unease was that he was being watched. Stephanie thought nothing about it at first, and carried on through lunch with little Jack in her arms. Callum ate his lunch, which to his delight, was animal-shaped sandwiches and a box of home-made cookies, inside a children's activity carry pack. Finger food was a favourite of Callum at lunchtime, it was simple and quick to serve to a hungry little boy.

Stephanie enjoyed Jack having his bottle in her arms. She took to motherhood quite well, although she was easily pleased when it concerned her children. When they were content she was content. It seemed as though she was never meant to be anywhere else but with her sons and her husband.

Stephanie leaned over to Richard and casually kissed him on the lips. 'Hey, have you noticed anything different today, Rich?' Stephanie sometimes called him Rich when she felt in a loving mood, it made her feel younger.

'Why, should I?' he said, looking bewildered.

In the far end of the restaurant, Stephanie had been sensing that Callum was still looking a little uneasy. He seemed to be watching someone or something. As Stephanie turned to look in the same direction, she saw a very tall elegant figure of a young woman slowly leave, but as the woman reached the doors she glanced back and stared directly towards them, as if to make sure they noticed her. Richard saw nothing but it seemed odd to him that Stephanie insisted it was definitely their table she had been staring at.

'Rich, that woman is staring at us. Do we know her?' She seemed irritated by the very idea. 'Rich, did you hear me?' But as she looked back again, the elegant figure had disappeared out of sight, and was no longer there when Richard turned his attention to Stephanie. He hadn't seen her at all, much to the distress of his wife, who by now was really quizzing who she could have been, or why she had stared at the family happy at lunch.

During all the fuss that Richard was oblivious to, Jack had gone to sleep after drinking only half of his bottle. Stephanie looked at the tiny little bundle and thought how angelic he looked. She placed him in his pram, gently stroked his delicate brown hair and gently tucked him in safely under the comfort of his little blankets. Callum had finished his lunch, so had Richard, but Stephanie had hardly touched hers as Jack had been feeding at the time. Not that she was hungry any more, as her mind was in another dimension. She simply had to know who that woman was.

The situation was beginning to get out of hand, as even

Richard wasn't aware of her distraction, but had he seen the woman in the doorway, he would have known what to say, or at least how to explain it. But he didn't see her and therefore there was no reason to share the dreadful secret he had hidden from Stephanie. After all, she hadn't found out or suspected anything other than the normal life she and Richard shared.

'Let it go, will you? What has got you so eaten up about this woman? I didn't even see her.' Richard wasn't too bothered at all and paid the bill and urged them to carry on with their shopping.

'I have to buy a new suit and a new briefcase for next week. Let's head to my shop first.' He said it was his kind of shop, but that had left much to be desired, as even Richard could only buy so many suits and it wasn't at all exciting for Stephanie, as she liked her labelled stores, and perfumes and expensive lavish taste that she had become accustomed to! Stephanie had many favourite stores and she longed to go to one and treat herself, but Richard had to get his suit so she decided to not be difficult and put up with the more serious needs of her husband.

'Mummy, can we go to the toy shop?' Callum was an inquisitive child and she was aware of how well he had come along. He was forward for his age since he had been six months old. He had been walking at ten months old and had begun talking by the time he was two years old. So it was hardly surprising when he asked a question.

It was a large toy store where Stephanie intended to take her sons, as she too loved all kinds of toys. They were a well-to-do family, they had built a nest-egg and just kept adding to it. They had worked hard to provide for a family, and now that Stephanie was no longer working, it provided very well for these occasions.

The law firm Richard was with was well known, and handled some very influential clients from all corners of the globe. It was a high-profile life in the law game. Richard liked the challenge, most his work entailed financial court battles and sometimes the odd case that he came across he would definitely fight for, even if he knew he would loose. But that was the challenge of being part of a law firm.

That was something that intrigued Stephanie. She liked a challenge herself and found it worth the long hours Richard was at work, just to wait for his return from a long day at the office. He liked to involve her in his work, they would talk for hours and discuss his cases well into the early hours of the morning.

Richard sensed that there were more urgent needs in the family other than his suit and ties etc. So he purchased what he needed and they left the store.

The family made their way to the only toy store that Stephanie regarded as 'the best', by which time Callum was getting really excited while his parents were talking to each other. He saw the large exquisite store in all its glory and was delighted when his parents stepped inside. Children have this extreme sense of spotting toy stores, and although Callum was only not quite three yet he knew a toy store when he saw one. Besides, his mother had taken him there before, when his little brother was still in her tummy. He hadn't forgotten what a magical place it was.

By now Stephanie had calmed down a little and had almost forgotten about the strange woman who had been staring at them earlier that afternoon. Richard stood watching Callum looking around the large toy department. Stephanie wanted to buy her sons everything in the store, but contained herself slightly as she didn't want to spoil them totally. Time flew by that afternoon as they lavishly charged their American express cards and visas. It was a truly extraordinary day, at the end of which they were all exhausted and excited, but pleased at how the day had gone. The boys were in the car by the time Stephanie had accounted the day's events.

Jack was sound asleep in his car seat and Callum was well strapped in, too. They were good boys and were sure to get a few surprises when they got home from their shopping trip. It was rare for them to make a family trip out of it, but today was an exception, as it was Jack's first major trip out shopping. It was very pleasant and exciting. It was the kind of evening in which the warm air on your face seemed just to gently brush softly against your skin, when the car window was down. The sun was just beginning to set in the distance and Richard commented on what a beautiful sunset it would be.

Rare moments like these were hard to come by in their busy lives. Some of his less fortunate friends didn't even have families, as they simply didn't have the time, their careers just simply would not allow it. Too much responsibility and hard work.

Suddenly the sun seemed to fade from before their very eyes. The road on which they were travelling home took a sharp bend and, before they knew what had happened, there was a sudden crunching sound, shattering glass and the boys began to cry uncontrollably. There had been a Porsche behind them most of the way home, and as they took the sharp bend the Porsche hit them from behind, sending their car reeling onto its side and almost onto its roof.

Stephanie couldn't move. Richard had miraculously almost escaped injury as the car had flipped onto the passenger side.

'Oh, my god, Stephanie! Stephanie, can you hear me? Are you hurt?'

The boys kept crying, not knowing what had happened. Both the children's seats were on their side, but at least they were making a noise. Stephanie was not moving. As Richard struggled to get out his seat, he leaned towards her. He saw blood on the side of Stephanie's head. She was unconscious and one of her arms looked broken and trapped.

There was no sound outside, only the wheels slowly spinning. Then there was a deadly silence all around.

'Daddy, Daddy, I want Mummy.'

Callum was very distressed, he didn't know what to say other than, 'I want Mummy.'

His tiny little brother Jack was screaming by that point and Richard tried in vain to get from his seat into the rear of the car to rescue his sons. Luckily it was easy to open his car door, although his window was smashed and the door dented, slowly he managed to remove his safety belt and eased himself out of the car. Richard's priority was his sons. Their door was jammed and wouldn't open, even with all his strength, so Richard had to calm Callum down and go back into the front seat again, and climb over to reach the boys.

Stephanie still hadn't made a sound or movement, he hadn't seen her beautiful body in this state before. He was terrified. At that precise moment it hadn't occurred to him to see what had happened to the other car. He didn't even know where it was or what it was that had hit him. They hadn't seen it. Richard began sobbing as he saw the two little car seats on their sides, not knowing what kind of state the baby was in, but knowing the children were still alive. He gently turned the first car seat back to its normal position and took his son's hand, and held it gently in his. Callum looked like a ghost, he was deathly pale, with tears running down his cheeks. It was then Richard knew Callum had only been shaken but not injured. Stretching over his seat, he could feel pain searing through his body, maybe he had a few broken ribs, but he had to get baby Jack out before worrying about himself. Using one hand, he pulled the infant's car seat toward him. Slowly he turned the screaming baby to face him. Jack's tiny face was red from screaming and his little legs were banging on his seat, and his hands were shaking violently and fists clenched.

But he seemed no more hurt than Callum. Releasing both their belts, Richard removed Callum and gently brought him onto his lap, and it was Callum who touched his mother, and gave the biggest hug to his father. He realised Mummy wasn't well. She wasn't moving or talking.

Richard eased himself from the wreckage and took Callum in his arms, and laid him by the roadside. 'Don't move, Callum. Daddy is just going to get Jack and Mummy. I am still here son, now be a good boy, and I will only be a minute.' Richard hesitated for a quick moment then left Callum.

Callum sat by the roadside waiting in shock, looking for his dad.

Every minute counted. There were no more cars around. Richard was able to bring Jack out in his baby carrier seat, so he didn't have to worry about where the two children were, while he tried to get Stephanie out. He placed the two brothers side by side, both seemed relieved to be able to see each other. Callum took Jack's hand and began to talk to his baby brother.

'Don't cry, baby, don't cry,' Callum softly whispered to Jack.

Because the car was on its side, it was more than obvious Stephanie was trapped in her seat. It seemed an impossibility as to how Richard was going to get his wife out of the wreckage. Stephanie looked so beautiful yet at peace, Richard knew she needed to get out of the vehicle as quickly as possible.

From out of the silence came a most welcome sound, the sound of other motors near by. As Richard began to emerge from the wreckage he saw two more cars on the accident scene. The passengers quickly rushed to the injured people, two of whom were the shaken, innocent little boys on the roadside. The drivers of the two cars assisted Richard at his car. They discussed several options, one of which was to push the car into its original state, back onto all four wheels.

Other passengers of the cars got out in shock to realise no one had come to the assistance of the vehicle that had gone into the back of Richard's car. It was just a few yards away behind the bend they had collided on, unknown to Richard. There was only one person in the car. She seemed to be in good shape, but was shaken. It was Stephanie and Richard who had had the full impact of the whole accident.

The car was slowly put onto solid ground and Stephanie still hadn't moved or even stirred from unconsciousness. All three men tried to open the passenger door, it seemed dented and stuck. One of the men went to his own car to find some kind of instrument or tool to loosen the door, and came back with a crowbar. This always solved the problem. It was the only way to get the door open.

As Richard intently prised the door ajar, Stephanie tilted towards him as it opened further. It was an intense moment for all who were involved. The flame-haired, beautiful woman was just sitting there without moving, stunned. She was still breathing but her pulse was faint. They eased her out of the car with relief and slowly laid her on the grass near her two sons, who stared in disbelief, not knowing what to say. Richard sat alongside Stephanie and the boys, and explained that Mummy was only sleeping.

In the nearby car came a whisper. The woman was in deep shock and unable to speak other than a whisper. One of the passers-by took his car and went to find a phone or help. It was a very isolated area the road they travelled. Everyone was being very helpful. A young man went to help the other woman and found that her car had minimal damage. The front of her car was smashed in but the rest of it seemed untouched. It was she who went into the rear of their car and, as hers was a car with a high-powered engine, it was the car in front that had come off worse. Porsches were resilient when it came to knocks and bangs or smashes.

'What's your name, love?' the young man enquired.

'Michaela Stornton.' She was conscious, but in deep shock. It was something this lady was not sure of at all. She was travelling alone in the car, but wasn't wearing any rings at all from what the young man could tell.

'Are you hurt? In any severe pain or discomfort?' Stupid questions, he knew, but they had to be asked.

'I feel bruised and sore on my chest and my arms but I'm okay really,' she said, slightly shy.

Her window had been wound down before the impact, so it was easy to make contact with her immediately. Sirens were in the background and a visible blue light seemed to appear at the scene. The police had automatically been informed on the 999 calls.

'Right what have we got?' Two officers were on the scene and were making immediate inquiries.

The passers-by were telling all they knew from talking to the injured parties involved. Richard was the first to be approached by a police officer, by which point the paramedic's team had reached them.

They were looking at Stephanie and were taking care not to hurt her as they placed her on a stretcher for the ambulance. This was a twisted turn of events as Richard still had shown no interest in the other car involved. He was too much involved with his own family to care, really. By now he was beginning to feel the shock. 'Is my wife going to be all right? She hasn't moved or opened her eyes since we, since we—' Richard began stuttering at that precise moment, and couldn't seem to get the exact words out before there was a reply.

'We are stabilising her, sir. I am doing all I can. Her vital signs look promising although she's unconscious, we can't find any permanent injuries other than her unconscious state.'

Both paramedics were men and very well trained. The first one turned to the two little boys and asked them their names.

Callum had to look to his father first before he was able to speak. After all, he'd always been told not to speak to strangers. 'My name is Callum, and my little brother is called Jack, he's a baby,' squealed Callum.

'Can I take a look at your sons, just to check them over, sir? They just need to be seen and checked for any slight injuries, although they look very well,' the paramedic said, looking straight at Richard.

'Certainly,' Richard said.

Trying to distract the boys proved to be a very social skill, as Callum asked one or two questions and Jack seemed interested in the lights all around him, as he'd never seen so many before. Time passed quite quickly and they arrived at the hospital within twenty minutes of the accident.

Stephanie was rushed from the ambulance and into the casualty department of the Medway General Hospital. She was in the best capable hands, and they would do their very best to help her. Richard was told to wait in the waiting room until they had seen her and treated her. But within minutes a nurse had been appointed to him to look over the two boys. They were luckily unhurt and were spoiled by all the nurses, as they looked so cute and innocent. This took Richard's mind off Stephanie for a while but he still felt anxious.

Jack had slowly drifted off to sleep in his father's arms, when a doctor came to the waiting room to let Richard know how his wife was. Callum was playing quietly with some toys in the corner of the room. He was so placid, he was never really any trouble to his parents. The doctor looked only to Richard and shut the door behind him. 'Are you Mr Sandlers?'

'Yes, I am, Doctor. How's my wife, Stephanie? She's okay, isn't she? She's not?'

The doctor could see what he was getting at and quickly shook his head and whispered, 'No, but we shall be keeping your wife here for some time, Mr Sandlers. She is in a coma. She has been unconscious for five hours now and we don't take that as a very good sign. On the other hand, she could wake up at any time.'

They had all been in the hospital for over four and a half hours now, and it was getting late for the boys to be out of bed. Stephanie usually bathed them both by 7 p.m. every night and would have tucked them into bed by now. But they were aware of how late it was.

'Can we see her now, Doctor?' Richard asked hesitantly.

'Yes, of course.'

Richard, still holding Jack, took Callum by the hand and followed the doctor down the halls of the hospital to a very quiet room. Stephanie was in intensive care for the time being, until they were satisfied with her condition. She had broken her right arm and was hooked up to an IV and was on different monitors.

She still looked youthful and very beautiful. Her bright flame-red hair shone all around her and almost glowing. She looked as though she was Sleeping Beauty from a picture book. Mummy is just sleeping, Richard thought, but would his sons really know how it was? She could be asleep for the next few hours or she might always stay in a comatose state.

What would he do without his beloved Stephanie?

He stood there, looking down at her in bed, and tears began to flow down his fair skin. How could this all have happened to them? he thought. Life at that moment seemed so unfair. Could he have been able to prevent the whole accident? More importantly, had it been his fault? What if she were to die because of him? The very thought racked Richard with guilt.

After consulting with the doctor, Richard gave Stephanie a sweet goodnight kiss on her lips and gently squeezed her hand in his, and then Callum kissed her too. Jack was long since asleep. He left a contact number at ICU and thanked all the staff. They would ring him if there was any change in Stephanie's condition.

Richard called for a cab from the casualty reception and went outside to wait. The cool evening air was refreshing and most welcome, as the hustle and bustle of bodies in corridors and injured people awaiting their doctors was beginning to seem very stressful. As the cab arrived outside, Richard and the boys sat back in the comfortable seats, and asked to be taken to their home, 9 Branor Close. It was a forty-minute drive. The county hospital had been the nearest to the accident scene. But the drive home was good and calming. Callum had been very well behaved and so had Jack. It gave Richard time to reflect on the day's events, and it had been just unbelievable. Not to mention poor Jack, who probably could do with a change of nappy and a warm bottle before bed.

He was on his own now, for the time being anyway. He would have to cope with the boys needs alone.

'What number did you say, sir?' The cab driver was quite pleasant, he could tell that there had probably been a family tragedy of some sort, but hadn't tried to pry unlike most cab drivers.

'Er, number nine, thank you,' Richard said, sounding totally exhausted.

'That will be twenty-four pounds, please.'

The cab then left and was heading down the end of the close as Richard fumbled for his keys. They all slowly walked in the door and waited just in the hall for a few moments, as if they were expecting Stephanie to follow them in at any moment, as though she was behind them. But she didn't come through the door, and Callum shut it as though he knew what they were all waiting for.

'Right then, boys, let's get you both something to eat and then I'll put you both in a warm bubbly bath. And how about a little story before bed?' Callum had insisted long ago that his baths were called bubbly and not bubbles, it was how he pronounced it, and it was what they called them now. Richard himself could have done with a good meal but settled for a snack with Callum.

In the meantime, he gave Jack a warm bottle of milk. Stephanie often had one or two prepared in the fridge. She hadn't taken them all in the baby bag for the outing. They had only been meant to be out for a feed or two at the most, no longer, as it had been Jack's first shopping trip and she hadn't wanted to be too long.

Unknown to her that was exactly what it had been, one long trip. Jack didn't seem at all fazed by the whole thing anyhow! He calmly took a full feed and was very content with that.

Their meal was ready too by this time and Callum was feeling quite hungry and pointed it out to his dad, who was just as hungry as he was. They sat down together at the breakfast bar and silently ate. It was as though they both knew what the other was thinking. Richard put his arm around Callum and assured him that everything would be okay, and that Mummy would be out of hospital very soon or at least he hoped she would be!

'Come on, boys, bubbly bath time.' Richard took the two weary little boys to the bathroom and gave them the bubbliest bath they had ever had.

'Lovely, bubbly,' chuckled Callum.

Jack was laughing also, he had begun to get used to the water now and seemed to enjoy it a lot. Jack was dressed in his babygrow for bed and lay on the bath mat, kicking his feet about and gurgling as Richard tended to Callum, who was not at all happy at having to get out of his bubbly bath.

But Richard persuaded him, and out he came, before long Callum was dressed in his pyjamas and also ready for bed. Callum helped his dad put Jack in his cot for the night, with his little blankets and musical light on. Jack loved his light as it reflected shapes and pictures around the room while playing a lullaby.

His mother had taken great care in decorating the nursery as she liked doing that kind of thing. It was a nursery to be proud of, with little delicate woodland animals in pictures and a lot of cuddly toys on a bean bag chair in the corner, and a beautiful rug on the floor, on which she would lay him to kick about. And it was full of brightly coloured toys and ornaments. And so Richard left Jack to sleep with all his comforts and slowly shut the door.

The baby monitor was switched on, so Richard didn't mind shutting the door as he could hear the baby anyway. Now it was time for Callum to go to bed and, although Richard was very exhausted, he let Callum choose a story and happily sat while Richard read to him. And when he'd finished, his dad gently tucked him into bed and left his little night-light on and assured him once more everything would be all right.

As Richard left the doorway of Callum's room, he realised he had to make the painful phone call to Stephanie's mother. Although he was sure she would not be awake, he had to call her immediately to tell her of her daughter's accident, and that now she lay in a comatose state at Medway General. It was 11 p.m., New York time, and that didn't make it any easier.

It had been a very traumatic day for Richard and Stephanie and their sons. But it was to be a harder one still for his mother-in-law, Frances Hayes. She was a very mature lady, and she was a well-spoken and intelligent lady who was adored by all her friends and family. She was a fantastic grandmother, one every child would wish for. She was on her own, as she had been widowed for some years. Harry had been long gone but her memory of him was still fresh. She had coped very well alone, and had lived in New York for a long time now. She only made visits to England two or three times a year, Christmas time and generally for a few weeks throughout the remainder of the year.

Richard decided to close the lounge door. He sat next to the phone and calmly dialled the numbers knowing Frances would be there. The wait was anxious as his line was being connected, it took just a few extra minutes. He heaved a heavy sigh and his heart missed a beat as he heard her voice.

'Hello.' She sounded fresh and cheerful. He knew that wouldn't be for long.

'Frances, it's Richard.' He sounded so nervous it terrified him to the bones. He had dreaded making this call, since the accident, but it had to be done. And now it was all so real. 'Frances, I have some news for you. I think you should know that I'm sorry but it isn't good news.'

Frances reacted immediately. 'Richard, what's wrong, dear? You sound awful.' He couldn't hold back anymore she knew there was something in his voice, but what was it? Richard began to sob uncontrollably and she felt her heart sink, the feeling you can't escape when you know you are about to be told something you really don't want to hear.

'It's Stephanie. She's in hospital, Frances. We were all in a car accident and now she is in a coma.' The words echoed down the line and it went so silent no noise, just silence. It was as though she was dazed. Richard had to speak again, not knowing how she was going to react.

'I'm coming over, Richard. I'll be there as soon as I can arrange a flight. Will she come out of the coma soon? What do the doctors say? How are you and the boys?' She had so many questions to ask, it was as though she couldn't ask them quickly enough. Richard replied straightaway, but he was concerned about her now. She was so far away and it would be a long trip for her to make on her own. Although she'd done it before, this time it was different. She would be in torment until her plane touched down in England.

Richard spoke to her and tried to give her as much information as he could, so she would feel prepared when she arrived. It was comforting in a way for both of them, as they both cared for the same people. 'The boys are shaken but we are all fine. We are so worried about Stephanie. They can't wake her. The doctors say she could be in a coma for quite some time. She is looking good, though, considering. I don't know a lot myself at the moment. I have just put Callum and Jack to bed, as it's been a very traumatic time for them. They don't really understand.'

It was late in the night for them and Frances knew he would have a lot to cope with over the next few hours. After all, her arrangements had to be made and pack, she wouldn't have been able to sleep anyhow. There was a five-hour time difference between their countries, and it was 4 a.m. here in England. 'Richard, I love you all so dearly. I wish I could be there right now to comfort you all, but I'll be there as soon as I can. I'll ring you back when I get my flight details organised, and you will know when to expect me. I can't believe this is my Steph we are talking about. Look after her for me until I get there, and give the boys a hug from me and let them know their grandma is coming to see them.' She sounded upset and very anxious, like Richard had when he called her. They both said their goodbyes and Frances told him how much she loved them all once again and would see them all very soon.

'Get some rest, Richard. You need to look after yourself too, you know!'

Richard agreed and said he'd see her soon, and placed the receiver back on the phone. If only she knew the truth, if only Richard knew! He had no idea who the other driver had been, and hadn't given it any thought to why it had all happened. But he soon would know all there was to know about who and why!

Chapter Two

Richard went to bed not long after the phone call, but couldn't even shut his eyes. He lay there awake for over an hour, just thinking about Stephanie, why she was the one who was seriously hurt and not him. He thought about looking after their sons and hoped he'd cope all right. After staring at the ceiling for so long, Richard finally showered and changed his clothes and went back downstairs. He sat staring up at the sky from the kitchen window until the dawn broke and the sunlight shone in his eyes so brightly he had to move across the room. The baby monitor had been switched on all night and Jack was still sound asleep.

Suddenly the phone rang and gave Richard a fright, as it hadn't rung since he came home the night before. It was Frances, confirming her flight. She was flying out of New York at 6 a.m. her time. She wasn't able to leave before then. Richard thanked her for calling and wished her a safe flight, and asked her to call when she landed at Heathrow later that day. Richard then called the Medway Hospital to find out some more on Stephanie's condition. There was no change, she was still comatose but they said she was holding her own, which meant she was a fighter and very strong-willed. They were comfortable with her condition, they described her as stable.

Jack had been awake for a little while by then, and lay in his cot gurgling and waving his tiny hands and feet in the air. He was a very placid and contented baby, never any trouble at all.

The children ate their breakfast that morning, wandering when Mummy was coming home, the trauma of the previous day still fresh in their faces. But Richard was fast finding out that children can be incredibly resilient. All the same he had to look at these two angelic faces and help them through this very difficult period of their lives. Callum was being particularly difficult when it came to getting dressed. Usually Stephanie encouraged him to try to dress himself, at least from his waist down. But Richard was being really understanding and offered as much support as possible. But this particular morning Callum refused to take his pyjamas off, never mind attempting to even as much as put a pair of socks on. While Callum was debating over the dilemma of whether to get dressed for the day or not, there was a loud knock at the door. So Richard came down the stairs with Jack still in his baby-grow and answered the door.

And there stood two policemen. They were in uniform and had a sense of urgency about them. Richard immediately turned a light shade of grey for an instant, at the impending thought of what they had to say.

'Hello sir, are you Mr Sandlers?' It sounded as though they were going to arrest him, from the look of them and how they addressed him, or so he thought!

'Yes, I am. May I help you, officers?' he inquired.

'May we come in for a moment, Mr Sandlers? We need some information on the accident that occurred yesterday afternoon.'

Richard now understood why they were here; they were following up on the information for the investigation into what happened. 'Yes, of course, please come inside. Please go into the lounge and sit down. I won't be a minute, I have my little boy upstairs trying to get dressed.' And he slowly shut the door and carried Jack back upstairs, to fetch Callum on the understanding that Callum could play next to Jack while he was in the playpen downstairs. He was to get dressed in a little while, when Daddy asked him. So they all came downstairs and diverted into the dinning room where the toys and playpen were. Richard left the boys to play safely and rejoined the two police officers, who were patiently waiting for him.

'Well, what can I help you with, officers?'

But it wasn't what Richard could tell the police, it was what they had to tell him that was to be of interest. 'I'm PC Darren Camp and this is my colleague PC Andrew Burton, Mr Sandlers. We have to ask you a few questions, if you don't mind, about yesterday?'

PC Darren Camp was the tallest of the two officers and obviously higher authority, compared to his colleague, who was the more perceptive of the two. They hadn't picked a good time to see

Richard as it was just after breakfast and he was trying to persuade Callum to get dressed, in order to be able to get things done. For example, Richard had to visit Stephanie and get updated on her condition. He also needed to go and see the wreckage of the car they had been travelling in at the time of the accident.

There were groceries to buy and laundry to do, and the usual day-to-day routine that Stephanie usually did while Richard was at work. All of which would have to wait until the police had finished their enquiries.

'We understand your wife is seriously ill in a coma. We are sorry to hear that.'

It was a short statement that led Richard to believe that they knew a lot more than he did.

'Thank you,' Richard responded, as though they knew Stephanie well.

'We are aware of the other driver and it is conclusive that the accident was not your fault, Mr Sandlers. It is now known that the lady involved, a Mrs Michaela Stornton, was behind the wheel of her Porsche, when she lost control of the brakes and failed to stop the vehicle before smashing into the back of your car.'

It sounded like something out of a horror movie. The name Michaela Stornton almost choked him as he sat opposite the two police officers, unaware he knew this woman.

As the truth revealed itself, Richard began to shake and hold his head in his hands. 'No, no.' His colour faded from his face and now he looked rather white in comparison to when the two policemen had arrived. Sweat began to seep through his skin and the officers began to notice how awful Richard now looked.

'Excuse me, Mr Sandlers, but are you feeling all right? You don't look very well.'

It was painfully obvious that what they had told Richard was of some shock to his system.

'It's okay, it's just I know that name. I know her personally.' Richard knew he had to offer an explanation, only lying about it would make it worse. So he had to tell the truth, whatever it was.

'Oh, I see, Mr Sandlers, is she? I mean, did you?'

They seemed to begin to know what exactly had been going on. 'It wasn't like that, Constable Camp. I assure you I didn't mean for it to happen.' He felt as though he was on trial in his own lounge. It was humiliating for these total strangers to know all about his infidelity. It was so hard for him to explain. It sounded like every other affair that had happened. But to them it sounded like another married man carrying on, and now he had been found out, with tragic consequences thrown in! 'I just can't believe it was Michaela in the Porsche. I had no idea. Is she okay?'

'She wasn't as badly injured as your wife, if that's what you need to know, Mr Sandlers.'

PC Camp had now got a clear picture of the whole thing in his head, and was wondering if the affair had maybe ended on a sour note. The very idea of an investigation being so complicated seemed too much to pass up, and so he decided to stick with the course of questions and pursue the case. Was it foul play or just purely an accident? That was the question on their minds now.

'What I mean is, I didn't mean for the affair to happen at all. The wrong time, wrong place, I guess. I'm married and I love my wife. Can't I be allowed to make one simple mistake?'

It was clearly a distraught man in an embarrassing situation amongst strangers, as he immediately tried to explain the whole situation. The two officers sat and looked interested as Richard poured his heart out.

'Is your wife aware of this affair?' inquired PC Camp.

'No, she isn't, and I would like you to let me be the one to tell her, when she wakes.' Richard knew it wouldn't be a pleasant experience. She trusted him and had never dreamed he would do a thing like this to her. He was feeling extremely anxious but they had more questions.

'Do you think there may be a reason why she was behind you on that particular road yesterday?' PC Burton asked subtly. It was a simple but relevant question, and he had to ask!

'I have no idea. She wasn't driving a Porsche nine months ago, the last time I saw her,' Richard said.

'Was there any animosity between you when you parted at the end of the relationship, Mr Sandlers?' By now, PC Camp was working on an idea that it had been a possible attempt on his life. Although it sounded as though Mr Sandlers had no way of knowing it was Michaela Stornton, she may well have known he

23

was in the vehicle in front!

At this point in the conversation, Callum came into the lounge, looking very impressed with himself.

The two boys had been very good, allowing their father to talk to the police in the lounge without any disruption. 'Daddy, look, dressed.' Callum was delighted. Richard threw open his arms to Callum and the small boy ran towards his father and giggled. It was a small accomplishment in a child's life, but it was the next step to doing more things for himself, and he knew daddy would need him to be good and try to help if he could.

'Good boy, Callum. You look great, kid.' His father praised him and showed a lot of affection, which was very much appreciated. 'Please excuse me, officers. I must go and check on my baby son Jack.' Richard disappeared into the dining room to see how Jack was. Jack was just lying there with a toy rattle in his grasp and gurgling away, and instantly gave a huge smile as his father's head appeared directly above his playpen. He looked so calm and unfazed by all that was going on around him on this particular morning.

When Richard emerged after a few moments, the two police officers were quietly whispering and taking notes about the conversation. Both had ideas and thoughts about the accident. 'Can I help you with any further inquiries, officers?' Richard asked without hesitation.

'I think we have all we need for the moment, Mr Sandlers. We will be in touch if we need any more information. Thank you for all your co-operation.'

Richard saw the two gentlemen officers out of the front door, and closed it with a heavy sigh. Now he could get on with things that needed doing. His day was to be filled with jobs around the home and taking care of the boys, and also the impending visit from his mother-in-law who would arrive later that day. Time was quickly going by and Jack still wasn't dressed. What would he do first?

As Richard slowly walked away from the door, a little voice said, 'Daddy, look.' His big blue eyes gleamed at Richard. Callum had put his jumper on the wrong way round but that didn't really matter. He was dressed and that was good.

'Well, if I say so myself, son, you look very smart this morning. Good boy.' Richard praised his son once more for how well he'd done. 'Shall we go and see if we can do just as good with Jack, with his clothes too, Callum?' It was something they could both do together. After all Callum felt pretty pleased with himself and he knew how socks and trousers went on too. So off they both went into the dining room where Jack lay in his playpen. Only now he had fallen asleep while waiting for Daddy to come and get him.

'Well, we will just have to try not to wake Jack, won't we, Callum? We don't want him to be grumpy. So let's be very careful and get him dressed just like you are!' Richard was trying to act how Stephanie would in a situation like this, and he was finding it all quite difficult by now! Slowly Richard lifted Jack from his playpen without waking him and gently put him down on his changing mat, next to Callum, who was already emptying Jack's entire nappy bag. Jack was well away, he lay there silently while Richard did a nappy change, and cleaned him down and dressed him. It was much easier to change Jack when he was sleeping than it was when he was awake, waving his arms and legs around. Richard was totally amazed at how gently Callum held his brother's tiny fingers and how lovingly he looked at his little brother.

Callum adored his little brother. He was also carefully watching his dad as he dressed his little brother. Jack showed no sign of waking up. He was dreaming and had a cute smile on his sweet little face.

Suddenly Callum began asking very difficult questions that Richard wasn't sure how to answer. 'Is Mummy coming home, Daddy?' It was an obvious question, though it didn't make it any easier for Richard. But he had to say something to his son.

'I don't think so. Mummy is having lots of sleep and rest in hospital at the moment. Hospitals make lots of people better all the time. And when Mummy is much better, she will be coming home to us.' Richard tactfully told Callum the truth and, as far as he was concerned, it was the right thing to say to his young and inquisitive son. Although honesty was not a problem, until the delicate subject of Michaela Stornton came to mind. But that was a matter he would have to deal with once Stephanie had recovered, as she would soon discover the truth. And that day was not one Richard had been looking forward to, since this whole mess erupted.

Jack decided to wake up before Richard and Callum had even put his socks on. Maybe the conversation had woken him up, but it didn't matter, as they would have to go out soon anyway. Richard glanced at the clock on the dinning room wall, and realised how much they had to do.

'Hello, Jack, didn't think you were going to wake at all until we had dressed you!' Richard gazed at his two sons and knew they were everything he ever wanted in his children. And now he was seeing a lot more of them, he absolutely loved every minute of it and Stephanie would be very pleased with him, he thought. But only for the way he was coping with their sons.

Callum thought he'd try to put Jack's socks on and Jack giggled as his big brother made the attempt, as Jack's feet were so much smaller than his own. It was a big enough job for him, and Jack was very ticklish on the bottom of his feet. He wiggled his feet so much even Callum began to giggle with his little brother. Richard sat on the floor playing with Jack and a few toys while Callum concentrated on the shoes. And Jack seemed contented.

'Right then, boys, shall we go and do some shopping for Mummy?' Groceries were at the top of the list that morning as Granny would be coming to stay with them, and they needed to make sure they would have everything they needed to make it a pleasant stay. Although she probably wouldn't be at the house much, Richard still needed certain items.

Richard searched the key rack on the wall in the kitchen for the 'not so family car', and he reached out for the Peugeot 205 keys. It was a small car but the boys would fit in as it was a four-door model. This was Richard's car. Usually, Stephanie would drive the family car, but the state it was in now, it was a write-off. At least he had his little car to fall back on. They would have to do the shopping first, as Frances wouldn't get all her luggage in otherwise. Considering Richard or Frances weren't sure how long she'd be staying, she'd probably bring quite a lot of her luggage. Their only pushchair had been in the family car, so Richard had to compromise and decide to make sure he put Jack in the shopping trolley with a baby seat until he could get another pushchair.

Jack was too big for his pram now. Stephanie had begun to use a stroller for Jack, but that was gone. At least he was aware of the problem. There was always a baby seat in the Peugeot, so that was a lot of comfort for the time being. By now it was almost 10.45 a.m., and they had to get going.

Richard pressed a button and the answering machine came on automatically. That way, if the hospital or Frances rang, they would be able to leave a message on the machine. Finally, they all bundled into the car and went about their urgent errands.

It wasn't exactly a pleasant morning, it had been raining and it was a bit muggy and damp. But all the same, they had to go out. There were a few people around doing their everyday things – the neighbours, most of who didn't have the faintest idea of what had happened to them in the twenty-four hours previously! No one seemed any different. No one questioned him as he left his home. Richard and Stephanie had always been polite to their neighbours, but they usually kept to themselves.

As Richard slowly turned out of the bottom of Branor Close, he realised it was the first time he'd been behind the wheel of a car since the accident, and he began to panic as to whether he could cope or not. Both his sons were in the car, they hadn't panicked at being inside another car or showed any fear at all. So Richard calmed himself down and took a deep breath and carried on driving. It wasn't easy but he had passed his first hurdle. As Richard took another left, he passed a familiar face that turned him very pale. He had seen Stephanie's best and favourite friend. She had known Stephanie since the age of seven. It was Laura Colt, she was petite with short brown hair. They had been friends for more than twenty years, and they had always told each other anything and everything that mattered. That was what friends did: they were each other's confidants to the extreme. They stopped just a few yards away from one another's cars on the opposite sides of the road. Laura opened her door and swiftly ran across to Richard's car.

'Hi, Richard, is Stephanie at home today?'

Richard hesitated as he looked at Laura, and she noticed

immediately.

'Richard, are you okay? You look very pale.'

He knew he had to tell her. All of a sudden he began to feel awfully guilty and ashamed of the whole incident. But he couldn't hide from it. 'Laura, Stephanie is in hospital. We were in a car accident late yesterday afternoon. She's in a coma, Laura, but she's not changed since they stabilised her.'

It was a lot of information to take in, but he told her and tears came to her eyes. It was painful for Laura to think of such a beautiful woman, so young, suddenly injured in such a way that she was totally relying on all resources to look after her every need! 'Oh, my god, Richard, where is she? Can I see her? Will she be all right?' Laura wanted to know everything, like Richard first had!

'She's at Medway, in ICU. They are doing everything in their power to give her everything she needs. We just have to sit and wait and hope it won't be too long until she wakes. You could go and see her and ask if you could spend a little time with her until we get there in a few hours.' Richard was hoping Laura wouldn't expect the whole truth and just accept it had been an accident, plain and simple.

The very idea of another reason for all this simply didn't come into the conversation at that particular time. But he wondered if she would find out more than he had bargained for.

'How are you and the kids? Were you hurt, too?' she asked, looking concerned.

'A bit shaken and a few bruises, but we seem to be okay. The boys don't realise the full extent of the accident.'

As she gazed into the rear of the car, she received gentle smiles from both of his sons. 'Okay, Richard, I'll catch up with you later. Have you rung Frances yet?' Laura quizzed, in a very polite manor.

'Yes, I called last night or, should I say, very early this morning. She's flying over and I'll be picking her up at Heathrow later this afternoon. She is absolutely frantic and worried out of her mind.'

'Bye, then, and I'll see you all later.' Her big brown eyes grew wider with despair. Laura then ran back over to her car, crying uncontrollably and shaking, not wanting to believe what she had just heard, the worst news about her friend. She sat in her car for what seemed like endless minutes and sank her head in her hands at the steering wheel.

Richard looked over and put out his hand to wave, but she wasn't looking, so he drove on. Concentrating was getting difficult, especially now that Laura was on the scene. She definitely disrupted the pattern of normality after that. Maybe she knew something was going on? And then she would tell Frances what she knew and side with Stephanie! Terrible thoughts began to plague Richard as he drove into the town. Questions he knew the answers to but no one else did. This whole mess is getting to me now, he thought. But it was the end result, the conclusion which he definitely had no control over!

'Jack, Callum, are you all right, boys? You're both very quiet this morning.' Richard was at a loss for words right at that moment. What would he say to them? Maybe they heard everything that had been said to Laura. After all, they were awake and in the same car as he was.

Callum looked subdued and sad. He stayed decidedly quiet until they arrived at the superstore. Then he broke his silence. 'Buy Mummy sweeties, Daddy, make her better.' His big blue eyes glaring at Richard made him feel very intense. His son was obviously disillusioned and not really understanding why his mummy was in hospital.

'Well, maybe flowers would be better, and your two smiling faces is what she really needs today, Callum.' The boy understood, he looked at his father and smiled and maybe things weren't going to be as rough that day as Richard first thought.

He drove into the rear car park of the superstore, and got out and paid the parking fee. They didn't intend on staying to shop for very long at all. He noticed immediately that the store catered for toddlers and babies in the same trolley, so it pleased all of them when Richard sat both the boys next to one another and began to stroll through the store. Jack was laughing and Callum looked at absolutely everything and pointed to certain sweets and biscuits.

It was usually a family shop but at least Richard knew what they normally put in the trolley. They all seemed quite at ease now and no longer nervous or subdued. They even managed to stop at the store's restaurant for a lunchtime snack before heading back home. Richard returned to his car with his shopping and sons in tow. They just managed to fit everything in the car. He turned the radio on and they left the car park in a good mood.

The sun had begun to peep through the grey sky, and seemed to brighten up the sky above. The next item on the list for the morning was to get a few things for Stephanie. He thought a new cassette that she was keen on might get past her unconscious state, as the medical staff called it. There were also other kinds of personal recollections that might bring her out of the coma. The sweet smell of Stephanie's favourite flowers that might help also, they were freesias. Stephanie had loved them for years and she adored their scent. That reminded him, he had to go to the local florist and buy a beautiful bouquet of as much as he could for Stephanie. But first he had to get to the other side of town. There was plenty on his mind to keep him occupied. He was sure he would remember everything. He bought his wife a beautiful gift set of a negligée and dressing gown to match, in a deep shade of champagne satin, and a few bedside bits and pieces for her to keep. There was little need for slippers in her condition!

Richard reached the florist and felt so guilty over Stephanie being in a coma that he lavished almost half the florist on her in her most favourite flowers. It made a slight improvement in his attitude. He knew guilt would not prevail, and his secret would be a secret no more. He declined the offer to have the bouquet sent by courier, Richard wanted to present them to Stephanie himself. Although he knew she couldn't see them, the scent would intimately reach her. If not the flowers, maybe her favourite singer, the female artist Sinead O'Connor might! Stephanie knew almost every word to every song she'd ever sang. And many songs she knew were tracks on the album she'd wanted for a while. She didn't have a taste for any other kind of music that Richard knew of, but she'd always liked the style of this particular artist and every song appealed to Stephanie's nature. Above all, Stephanie was quite a good singer herself, although she never showed her talent anywhere other than in the home. Maybe when this was all over, she might well do something about it!

But this was the future he was thinking about, it was now he had to deal with. Her friend Laura had probably reached Medway by now, and comforting her lifelong friend. Laura had looked absolutely devastated by what he'd told her earlier that morning. As he drove home he couldn't get the image of Stephanie in hospital out of his mind, then suddenly he realised, what if she were paralysed and wouldn't walk again? What if she was in a wheelchair for the rest of her life? He couldn't cope with that. That sounded very selfish, but knowing he was all right didn't make it any easier. If anything, it would make his life so much harder than ever before. He just couldn't comprehend the meaning of it all. There was also the issue of work, he had to call them and explain the situation and that he would have to take some time off. He was sure they would understand, and allow him the time for personal reasons.

The drive home was pleasant. Callum sat in the back talking small talk with Jack, who was grasping one of his toys. They had behaved well for Richard and he really did appreciate it as he was sure deep down they knew things were a little different and difficult, and Daddy was trying hard to do things without their mother.

They arrived back at Branor Close shortly after 2 p.m. and he still had many things to do. Besides which, Frances would need picking up at the airport in a few short hours. Richard carried Jack into the house and Callum followed behind. He sat Jack in the playpen and went back out to the car to unload the shopping. There was plenty to carry inside and Callum helped carry some of the items, which helped tremendously. Little helping hands do share the work, Richard thought to himself.

There was a bleeping sound coming from the phone and Callum quickly pointed it out. So Richard finished what he was doing and went to find out what the message was on the machine. It was Laura, who had called an hour previously to let him know that nothing had changed and she was allowed to stay by the bedside of her best friend. She told Richard she'd be there for as long as it was okay with the nursing staff. There was no problem and Richard was relieved to know someone would be there to be near Stephanie and talk to her until he arrived with Frances.

The boys hadn't yet seen their mother since the previous day and it wouldn't be easy for them, either. But for now Richard thought it best that they see her when they had time to come to terms with what happened to her. They would think she was asleep, but would expect her to wake up, and he knew he couldn't bear to see the pain on their faces when they knew what was really happening. So Richard turned the message off and calmly walked out of the lounge and into the kitchen to help Callum put the shopping away. There were lots of small items Callum could help with, packets of biscuits and crisps and so on. He wanted to be useful and help his father as much as possible.

Richard left the flowers in the car so they weren't handled too much. It was cool in the car now anyway. He didn't want them to look any different than the way the florist arranged them.

Richard was sure Stephanie would be charmed by their scent. Now all Richard had to do was wait for Frances to call from the airport. It would only take him an hour to get to the airport and the boys would be delighted to see her, as she would be to see them. But she wasn't expected to call for another hour when the phone rang and startled Richard. He quickly paced into the lounge and hesitantly picked up the phone. There was noise in the background as Richard said hello to the person on the other end of the line. Then he recognised the noise, it was coming from the arrival lounge at the airport.

'Hi, Richard, it's Frances. I've just landed. I arrived on time and I had a safe trip.'

'Hello, Frances, very pleased to hear you've arrived safely. I'm on my way. Stephanie's condition hasn't changed, but she's stabilised. They watched her constantly through the night. And Laura came by, I told her everything and she's keeping a vigil by her bedside as we speak. I'll get to you as soon as I can.'

The conversation went very politely.

'Okay, Richard, see you in a while, I'll be in the restaurant when you arrive. Bye for now.' Frances was satisfied to hear Richard's update, and didn't ask anything more. She had heard all she needed to know.

Richard placed the phone down and shouted Callum through. First Callum just looked his father in the eyes and then jumped with excitement at the thought of his grandmother visiting. He had to give the boys a quick snack and wash and change of nappy for Jack. Then they could leave for the airport. Frances had called earlier than expected, but at least she had arrived safely.

It had started to rain again, the weather was really unpredictable that day but that didn't really bother Richard. Callum had asked to wear his new wellingtons, even though he was going to be in the car more than outside in the rain. These wellingtons were special, they were green with frog eyes on the front and Callum really loved them. Stephanie had taken him to the shop where he had seen them and bought them for him. So this made them very special wellingtons.

So Richard allowed Callum to wear them in the car. They had managed to salvage most of the goods they had purchased on that fateful afternoon, from inside the wreckage, although just seeing the smashed-up wreck was painful enough. And of course Callum got his wellingtons back. Jack went to sleep as soon as Richard had changed him, everyone was fed and refreshed and they were on their way.

Chapter Three

They pulled out of the drive once more and left Branor Close again. The rain was really pouring down now and Jack was still asleep. He didn't have much time for play, he either slept or ate or was in the car with his father and brother and, when he was at home, he would be in his playpen or in his cot. But to a four-month-old baby time didn't matter anyway. Richard played a tape in the car of children's favourite games and songs, which passed the time for a while. Callum was in really high spirits and that cheered Richard up.

They reached the airport in good time and parked in the pick up area at the arrival and departure lounge. Richard was allowed twenty minutes in that space and took the boys in search of Frances. There were lots of people rushing around and noises coming from inside the airport. Callum was wide-eyed and took notice of all the travellers. Jack was slumped across Richard's shoulder, and was blissfully unaware of what was going on around him. Sometimes Richard thought Jack would sleep through absolutely anything, nothing ever seemed to wake him.

Richard and Callum reached the arrival lounge and walked through towards the restaurant area, looking for Frances, hoping at least she hadn't changed her hairstyle. After all, she hadn't visited since Jack was born and now he was four months old. And over in the far corner was a very smart charming older woman dressed in a very flattering navy suit. Of course, it was Frances Hayes, his mother-in-law. Boy, she knew how to dress elegantly, but then she always was a lady with a lot of class. They saw each other and waved. They met each other in the centre of the room, and just hugged one another for a very long moment.

Tears filled her eyes as she looked to the young family standing before her, and where her daughter should have been standing was a big empty space. 'Oh, Richard I'm so sorry. I've been very worried during my flight, thinking of you all. I haven't stopped praying for Stephanie to come out of this coma and be with her family again.' She spoke with such dignity and loyalty for her daughter. She was hurt and it showed. She contained herself for the moment, but she was sure to break down sometime that day!

'Let's go to the car Frances, you look very tired and worn out. It's been a long day for all of us.'

They made their way out of the airport and out to the parking area, where their parking time was almost up anyway. It had stopped raining, which disappointed Callum as he had his new green wellingtons on and he wanted to splash around a bit before the puddles dried up. But there wasn't time anyway. But it was good to see grandma again and he'd really grown up since she last saw them both. Jack had woken by the time his father had placed him back in his tiny baby seat. And when he saw his grandmother he let out a tiny squeal and with delight grinned blissfully at her.

'Wow, that was a surprise, Jack, you little cutie. You've got your mother's smile.' And that remark let a tiny single teardrop fall upon her cheek and roll down to touch her dark pink lips. It was heartbreaking, the pain in her face as she realised the words she had just said.

'Eh, Frances, would you like to sit in the front or in the back with Jack?' It was obvious now that the whole mess had really got to her and it would be a difficult journey home in the car.

Although she knew Stephanie was in the best place, it still didn't make it any easier. She was in a coma and no one knew how long she would be in that state, in intensive care. But these were facts they were aware of. She glanced again at Richard, who was obviously waiting for a reply, and she turned her head and looked at Jack. 'I would very much like to sit with Jack please and get to know my grandsons a little more.'

'That's fine by me, Frances. I'll pop Callum in the front with me.' He swiftly removed Callum's seat from the rear and put it in the front.

The boys were both safely strapped in their car seats and ready to go. Frances sat quietly next to Jack and Richard bundled all her luggage into the tiny boot of the car. Trying not to touch the beautiful bouquet on the back shelf, he shut the boot and walked around the side and got into the driver's seat.

'They're beautiful flowers you've got there, Richard. Stephanie is sure to know they are there.'

She was getting choked up by now, Richard just reached out and touched her hand and then started the engine up. Slowly they drove out of the airport terminal entrance, and began the journey home. Frances was quieter than he'd expected. She didn't ask any questions or made any accusations as to whose fault the accident was. She just sat there, listening to Jack gurgling away. It wasn't until they were almost home that it dawned on him that someone would have to be with the boys that afternoon when they went to the hospital.

As he pulled up in front of the house, Laura's car was parked alongside the drive. She was sitting inside and looked like she'd been there a while. Why was she here? Was Stephanie okay?

'Don't panic, Richard, Steph's all right. I just dropped by to see if there was anything I can help with.'

Frances emerged from the car, and the emotion between the three of them ran really high. There were tears, and there were smiles. It was a rich moment of togetherness and warmth and strength. They felt needed and very much united. They welcomed each other and all of them went into the house. Laura and Frances sat in the dining room for more than an hour, just talking and trying to grasp the reality of Stephanie's condition. Then Richard walked in with the tea tray for everyone, and in came Callum bounding behind him. Jack was seated in the baby chair on the floor and Callum sat next to him, holding a bottle for him.

Frances turned to Richard and began to talk very generally about what happened. She wanted to be very much in the knowledge of things, when she arrived at Stephanie's bedside. Richard just basically explained the journey home and what came next; he didn't want to be too graphic, as the boys were so close by and very much unsure about the whole incident. But as the facts began to unravel themselves, no one at all began to suspect anything was being hidden from them.

If the truth was known, Richard began to feel as if Frances and Laura felt sorry for him and the boys. How could he tell them what he knew when they were giving him all this sympathy? And he wasn't feeling at all guilty by now whatsoever! In fact, what did guilt have to do with it? No one really had to know, not yet anyway. At which moment, the conversation turned to Laura and she quietly pointed out to Richard that if he needed a sitter for the children at short notice, she would be there for him.

Richard kindly took up her offer and Laura decided to stay the rest of the evening, while Richard and Frances went to visit Stephanie. Frances took her overnight holdall and disappeared upstairs to freshen up. And Richard and Laura discussed the boys. Richard explained their routine and bedtimes. There were never usually any problems. He noted the Medway ICU number so she could reach them. They were not looking to exhaust Stephanie as they wanted her to keep it as stress-free as possible. Visits were usually not too long in ICU for these cases anyway.

Richard sat and played with his sons for a short while before going upstairs to freshen up himself before leaving to visit his wife. He hadn't seen her at all properly since they took her in the ambulance to the hospital and he had only seen her for a short time before he brought the boys home. While he was upstairs, he went into the boys' bedrooms, and looked out a clean pair of pyjamas for them both. And then, as he went to go into his own room, he heard a whimpering cry. He slowly walked towards the bathroom and as he walked to the door the crying stopped. It was as though Frances knew there was someone else there.

She sniffed as she opened the door, and peeked her head out. There, just a few yards away, was Richard, looking bewildered. He thought she was really keeping it together and intact. But he knew she would break some time. And it looked like it would be sooner than later. 'It's only me, Frances. It's okay to have a little cry. It's a lot to cope with in such a short time. Maybe you'll feel better once you've seen Stephanie.'

'I suppose this is the last thing Stephanie needs, me crying every time I look at her. I don't want her to be thinking I'm no good in emergencies or a crisis. I need her to know I'm there for her, and I want to do anything I can to help her.'

It was a time to reflect and consider others' feelings. Indeed they didn't know what lay ahead. The first trip to ICU would be a difficult one, they knew that. They both stood in the hallway and shared a hug and sighed, and then wiped the tears away. And Frances left Richard to get ready while she went downstairs to see the precious grandsons she so dearly adored.

As Stephanie was an only child, Frances treasured her family. They were all she had now as her husband Harry had been deceased for some time. Frances was on her own now in the States; apart from her friends over there she had no one. They had moved out to the States when Stephanie was a little younger. It had always been a dream of theirs to retire to the States. They'd made a good choice, a new lease of life for them, a different experience. But then Harry had passed away and left her alone.

Stephanie was a tower of strength and really comforting when Frances needed it most. They were good together, Frances and Harry. But it was good to listen to her reminisce and talk about the good times with Harry, sadly Richard had never got to meet Harry. They were what counted, the good times; good times came again when Stephanie announced she was to marry Richard. And the sun certainly shone when they told Frances she was to become a grandmother. It was just a shame Harry couldn't have shared the celebrations of those very special occasions.

The boys were the light of her life and changed her view of loneliness totally. Stephanie and Richard had even offered to have her come over and live with them when Harry died. But she quickly declined their offer, as she felt as though her roots were in New York now. She'd retired out there and Harry was laid to rest out there, so she didn't want to leave. But it was good to visit and see the children. She felt she belonged near Harry. She had made her home in New York and that was it.

Although she was miles away, she kept in constant touch with the family. The only family she had and they meant the world to her. But now it was the very reason she'd flown out in such urgency. Frances composed herself, sniffed a little and told Richard she'd wait downstairs for him and then they would leave. It was only a few minutes when Richard came downstairs, wearing a casual look of jeans and a polo shirt. He had always been a smart dresser. That was one thing that caught Stephanie's eye at times, especially at that dinner party on that particular evening. Frances thought he was a good catch, too, but she'd never really said. But she knew they were good together, and to her she just wanted her daughter to be happy. And to this day she thought they were the perfect couple.

'Okay, I'm ready, Frances. Just let me say goodnight to the boys, as they should be in bed when we get home.' And as he poked his tall, slender figure around the door, Laura smiled at him. He watched his two boys just lying there on the floor and playing around with some of Jack's toy soft building blocks.

'They'll be fine, Richard. Just go and give Stephanie a big hug for me. Oh, don't forget the elegant nightgown you bought for her; I know she'll like it.'

Richard bent down, kissed the boys and left the room as he had entered without any sound. The boys were in no way distressed and were quite content with their babysitter for the evening. 'Right, let's go!' Richard grabbed his keys from the small key-rack on the kitchen wall, and made his way to the front door past Frances. He picked up the small carrier bag that contained the nightgown for Stephanie and a few other bits and pieces he had gathered, and opened the door; Frances went first.

The flowers were still very fresh and still looked beautiful. It was late afternoon now, around 5.45 p.m. and as they drove to the bottom of the close Frances began to feel her heart beat just a little faster than it did usually. She felt very anxious and a little faint, but she didn't mention it at all to Richard.

Richard asked if she was okay, she looked a little pale, but she nodded her head and looked out of the window. They arrived at the hospital just after 6.20 p.m. and they parked at the back of the building, where spaces were available to park for longer periods of time.

'Richard, I'm just nervous at what I will see when I see Stephanie. It's hard for me; she's still my little girl and I guess I'm just frightened of losing her.'

'We'll get through this together, I promise. Stephanie is going to need us both to be strong. And we are, aren't we?'

Richard looked at Frances and smiled, she smiled back and put a hand on his arm and told him she'd be fine. The sound of an ambulance siren interrupted the calmness in the air. And they both emerged from the car not knowing what to expect at ICU.

The hospital was buzzing with life, and doctors with pagers and white coats. The bright lights were very daunting and the scent of meal trolleys and the smell of surgical cleanliness was flowing through the air. They both waited for the lift; as the doors opened the look of some of those faces was so depressing, Frances felt as if she would burst into tears right there. The feeling was so overpowering. There was just enough room in the lift to take them, the lift stopped at two more floors before people began getting out.

The ICU was on the third floor and you could hear a pin drop all the way to the end of the corridor. Frances had been carrying the big bouquet of flowers from the car and the fragrance brushed her face and made her smile. It would be pleasant to have by a bedside. They were beautiful and Richard had made a good choice.

They were also the same flowers Stephanie had had in the church for her wedding. The church had been filled with the aroma of freesias. It was a wonderful memory. Richard took Frances's arm and they both looked for the sign with the words INTENSIVE CARE UNIT, and followed the directions. They quietly walked with their own thoughts.

It didn't take long to reach the unit. There were swinging doors that led to the ward, and as they walked through they had to report to the nurses' station and ask to see the particular patient they had come to visit. There weren't any doctors on the ward but one would be available to speak to them later. But they were cleared to visit any one patient at one time.

The nurse in charge was a staff nurse, Olivia Henson; she was brilliant. She showed Stephanie's husband and her mother into the room, briefing them as they went in. She would be in the ward all evening.

It was one of the most intense moments Frances had ever encountered. The same woman who shared both these lives was lying so still, it was horrifying. There she was, so beautiful and elegant, but at the same time she was comatose and it was hard to believe. She was hooked up to an IV drip and a heart monitor. She was in the care of a very capable work team of nurses on the unit and had one-to-one nurse care. Her vital signs were looking good but she might not make a full recovery, which was a very uncertain future they might have to account for.

Richard gently urged Frances to sit on an easy high-backed chair next to her daughter's bedside. And he followed her, sitting a little further down the side of her bed. The nurse walked over to where they were sitting and offered some information about how to communicate with Stephanie, and she also pointed out how beautiful the bouquet was, and it should go directly into a vase of water. She was very pretty and looked suited to her job. And she was certainly very helpful.

Olivia left the unit with the fragrant flowers in one hand, while Richard followed her advice and requested a tape recorder. Well, it was worth a try; maybe the sound of familiar music of Stephanie's favourite tunes might trigger a response. They were also told to talk and laugh as though she were awake and could communicate back. It was very difficult to begin with but then, when they knew what to talk about and how funny some stories were, Frances and Richard began to get into the swing of things. Olivia returned with a beautiful vase and mentioned how she managed to fit all the flowers in it, and connected the tape recorder up for Richard.

'Do you mind my asking what Stephanie's favourite music is?' She didn't want to sound too nosy but just interested.

'Stephanie actually loves the female singer Sinead O'Connor, she's her all-time favourite singer. Stephanie's so in touch with the feeling and rhythm of her music.'

It was an accomplished statement, but Richard felt strongly about how well he knew his wife and he could sense that Olivia was closely studying him. Richard began to play one of the albums Stephanie had in her collection and quietly played her some songs.

An hour had passed by and Frances was now getting used to the whole situation and felt quite at ease now. She knew her daughter was not in pain but looked suspended in a deep sleep. Olivia appeared at the foot of Stephanie's bed and began to look at her medical notes; she then proceeded to look at the monitor and the IV drip. Nothing had changed but she needed to check constantly for any changes. She sat on the bed next to Richard and told him the case doctor would be along shortly to check his patient. His name was Dr Rosenstein, and he would fill them in on any details they wished to be updated on, and true to form he arrived only fifteen minutes later.

He was a very tall gentleman and very distinguished-looking, with silvery white hair. He could easily be near retirement age but looked very confident.

'Hello, Mr Sandlers, I'm Dr Rosenstein. Your wife is making steady progress but don't confuse me with recovery. She is simply very comfortable and stabilised. She had a broken right arm, but no other injuries apart from her present condition. Mrs Sandlers is connected to both an IV drip and a heart monitor, as you can see. Both show stable conditions. Your wife was given a CT scan almost instantly on arrival and we are pleased there is no permanent signs of any brain damage. Basically, she is in a coma and it's just a matter of time as to when she comes out of it.'

'Dr Rosenstein, what else can be done for my daughter while she is in this condition?' Stephanie's mother was inquiring what kind of treatment was being given to Stephanie.

'Mrs Hayes, I assure you everything possible is being done for your daughter. We are giving Mrs Sandlers muscle therapy, in which Nurse Henson gives her intense muscle massage so her muscles are kept active, by rubbing oils into her legs and arms so she isn't weak when she becomes active again. This procedure is done twice daily and it also encourages movement, which prevents any soreness and stiffness due to immobility. It also stops her skin from drying out.'

It was just what Frances wanted to hear. Her daughter was being well cared for and they couldn't expect any better treatment than what she was receiving. Then came the most important question: Frances had to ask, to know what to expect!

'Dr Rosenstein, may I ask you a very important question? How long is my daughter going to be in a coma?'

Richard looked at Frances, very startled. He hadn't expected to hear her ask such a thing. But he understood she had to know.

'Well, I'm afraid I really can't be precise with an answer. You see, when someone is in a coma, it's a very deep sleep in which there is no control over the body's reactions. I'm being honest with you both now. Your daughter and your wife could be in a coma for the minimum time of a few days, but the downside is she could be in this state for a possible five to ten years. We have no control whatsoever; it's all up to the patient and their will power and determination to survive.'

It was an abrupt conclusion to a well-put question, but it couldn't really give them an answer that they really wanted.

'Well, thank you, Doctor. I understand the situation you are in, it can't be easy having to tell relatives this kind of information. We all have faith and I'm sure when she is ready Stephanie will come back to us,' Richard said politely.

'In the meantime you can talk and laugh and tell her all about the events from her past and the good times. Music is also good to let her hear, as most patients are aware of sound, noise and voices, even if they cannot respond to let you know they can hear you. As I can see, you came prepared.' Dr Rosenstein shook hands with both the husband and mother and said goodbye. He would be back later that evening before his shift was to end to check on her.

But to Richard the doctor was impressed with all her vital signs. He pointed out Staff Nurse Henson would arrange for them to be given a cup of tea. They had been there for a little over two hours and needed a drink. The evening had passed so quickly.

Stephanie lay there with her flowing bright-flamed hair; she still had a fair complexion and just a few freckles over her nose that made her look so cute. 'I suppose I had better bring Callum and Jack in to see her as she needs to hear their voices, and they aren't really understanding why she's not at home.'

He knew he was right, but there were to be more delicate decisions ahead for him to tackle. His mother-in-law nodded. She hadn't spoken much throughout the evening, due to the shock of what had happened. Richard knew Stephanie was listening.

Suddenly Richard was aware of the heart monitor bleeping, and it startled him as he stood there staring at it. Now it seemed real and it hit him hard in the face. This was reality and it wasn't going to change for anything. Life had this way of being a pack of cards, it dealt its hand and you either came up trumps or took a dive! Richard had come to accept this way of life and live with the blow that fate had dealt him, but he was going to cope with this the best way he knew how. Richard bent over his sleeping wife and gently kissed her lips. She felt warm and delicate. He could still smell the sweet aroma of her perfume, as if she had freshly sprayed it on that day!

He knew everything about her; her life was his! He believed in her, that she would get better and things would be as they had been. He stood up tall and stretched, looking over at Frances who was now beginning to close her eyes with tiredness. Maybe it was time to leave Stephanie to rest and they could go home and do the same. It was getting late and he had almost forgotten Laura was babysitting. It was an extraordinary day, and the stress was relieving itself at last. At least they knew more than they had that morning. It would be a little more bearable from this point onwards. Who knew what tomorrow would bring? Tomorrow was a new day. So Richard gently touched Frances's arm and whispered they should go home. Nurse Olivia was still monitoring Stephanie and there was no change.

They thanked her for all her help and said that they would return again the next day.

'We will take care of her every need, Mr Sandlers,' said the pretty nurse; her looks hadn't gone unnoticed. Even Frances had remarked how pretty she was on the way down in the lift. But it was just something to talk about, to keep away from the subject of what may happen to Stephanie if she didn't make it.

The hospital was beginning to wind down and almost all the visitors had long gone. It was almost silent. The lift reached the ground floor and the doors opened to expose two exhausted people just standing there, silent and pale. It had been the most extraordinary twenty-four hours of his life.

When they arrived home, the boys had been well looked after and put to bed. Laura had cleaned up after them and looked very worn out herself, but she had said they were no problem and it was a really enjoyable evening with Callum and Jack. She left soon afterward and headed home.

A week had passed much as the weekend had and it seemed as it had been an eternity since that awful day. There was no such change to make any difference and Richard began to question his faith, as to what the future held for him and his wife. How many more weeks could he take this for? Could he be in for years of suffering and uncertainty? When would it all end? His strength had never been put through such a challenge.

The visits carried on, some with his sons, some on his own. The boys coped quite well. They accepted she was sleeping and she would come home one day! Until then the music played and the stories were told and Laura made lengthy visits to reach out to her pal, her best friend, her confidante. She didn't want to lose all that, as they had been so close for so many years.

Richard was still into routine at home and the boys were behaving fantastically and Richard was enjoying all the time he had with his sons. Frances was such a big help and her experience was really appreciated. She was a good grandmother and had such a way of telling bedtime stories that Richard began to listen in on them occasionally. The boys loved her dearly and she kept their little minds off their mother when she thought it necessary!

Richard had been given the all clear on as much time off as he needed. It was yet another tiring day and on this particular occasion Frances had taken some time out for herself when Richard went to the hospital. She stayed in bed a little longer than usual and phoned to see how Stephanie was while still in bed! She heard nothing new about her daughter's condition, she later planned to go shopping and relaxing to take all the recent events into account.

Richard sat the boys in the back of the car and drove steadily to the Medway hospital. It was a very sunny day and the boys were full of delight at visiting their mummy, although each time he walked into ICU he never knew what to expect. The boys got more and more excited as they approached the hospital.

'I want to see Mummy, I want to see Mummy,' Callum declared.

There was so much change in their sons. They seemed to understand and know how their daddy was feeling. If Richard looked sad and unhappy, which many a time he did, then they were usually quiet and behaved very well. And there were pleasant times when they sensed the happiness and peaceful feeling and they were smiling and giggling and playful.

Today was a good day. Richard felt it was going to be a good day as soon as he woke up. Richard made decisions like that most mornings. It was just the way things happened. They parked and the boys just couldn't contain themselves any longer; Callum leaped out of the car like a bolt of lightening! His father reached out to stop Callum from running into the middle of the car park. Jack was still waiting to be released from his car seat. Callum had calmed down a lot by the time Richard sternly told him to behave!

They walked into the hospital casual and smartly. Richard was sure the boys would have lots to say to their mother. People were all in the corridors and it seemed much busier than the previous visits. Up they went in the lift and through the same corridors leading to the Intensive Care Unit. Staff Nurse Henson was once again on duty. She was at the desk catching up on some paper work from through the night. Her job was very complex, as she was a one-on-one nurse with a particular patient at any one time, and also she was a senior staff nurse in charge of another team of nurses and there was a lot of paperwork involved too. It wasn't easy for her but she was well regarded and respected among her fellow colleagues.

The boys could hardly wait to talk for their pure excitement as they entered the ward, where Olivia was sitting. She smiled at the two inquisitive young faces staring back at her. She pointed them in the direction of a particular bed, which was their mothers.

They couldn't see Stephanie from the height they were but she was behind a private curtain. Richard made mild conversation for a few minutes and then took Callum's hand and they walked a few yards to Stephanie's bed. Jack was still in his dad's arms and was gurgling away in his own unique language. Slowly Richard approached the bedside of his wife and swiftly pulled back the curtain to reveal Stephanie's beautiful slender figure beneath the bedding. Her wonderful red glowing hair flowing down her face was breathtaking, a sublime image to look upon! Her face was pale, but the freckles seemed to give her complexion some colour.

Callum looked amazed and immediately touched his mother's face with his tiny hands. He smiled and gently leaned over to kiss her with a butterfly kiss that was so gentle she probably didn't feel it at all. His face seemed to look as though he understood. Daddy had told him Mummy was sleeping; she had been asleep for some time but she would be okay.

They all sat on a few chairs and Jack began to get slightly restless. Mummy wasn't picking him up or talking: why? He couldn't understand like his brother, but he knew who she was and he recognised her instantly. The way they adored their mother was real love from such youngsters. Richard touched Stephanie's face and whispered, 'I love you,' in her ear.

All three of their faces were constantly watching the monitors and Stephanie in her bed. The room was almost silent but for the bleeping of the monitors, and the children's voices. From time to time the boys would giggle while Richard spoke to her, constantly touching her face and hands. He wanted her to know in any way, he was there for her and so were the boys! He wasn't sure if the music had done anything for her, so he began to talk of their sons and what they had been up to at home. There were funny stories to tell and especially the fact that Laura had been and babysat for them. She'd had a good time and she took care of their every need. But they had fun and that's mainly what counted.

Suddenly there was a very slight movement in Stephanie's eyes. Although they were closed all the time, there was a flicker. It made Richard jump, as there hadn't been any reaction or movement in two weeks at all! He watched her religiously now to see if she did it again, and she did.

Stephanie was actually making the smallest of movements.

Richard shouted to call Olivia over to the bed. She should see this; it looked so good for Stephanie to be making some kind of progress. Olivia quickly moved from the nurses' station to Stephanie's bedside. She immediately took Stephanie's pulse; her pulse rate had slightly risen and her vital signs were still stable. The heart monitor was stable, not yet showing any reaction. Richard was still holding her hand when he felt a tight squeeze between his hand and hers. It was an intense moment and exciting, too. Olivia saw the hand move too and made a call to have Dr Rosenstein come immediately. This was a tremendously nervous time for all involved. Comatose patients had no time limit to when they would eventually wake up; you couldn't predict their recovery.

Dr Rosenstein was on the scene of ICU almost instantly. He

took Richard to one side while Olivia looked after the two boys; he warned Richard that now Stephanie was showing recovery signs that anything could be possible. Just hoping that she would totally recover and not relapse, which hadn't been ruled out at this point!

'Will she be okay, Dr Rosenstein? She will be able to walk again?'

No one knew the answers, not yet anyhow. It would take time and patience. Now she was waking she would have to be monitored more intensely and probably eventually have another brain scan to detect any abnormalities. But for the moment it was good to see things happening at last.

It was getting busy with all the nurses around the ward and several people tending to Stephanie. Suddenly she opened her eyes as Richard approached her bedside. And he was the first person she saw at that moment. And she smiled at him with so much love. It was obvious that they loved each other so much.

What was even more special was he had been in the right place at the right time; this time he was with his wife when she needed him most. Stephanie looked dazed as she tried to focus on the bright lights and all the faces surrounding her. After all, she had been unconscious since the accident happened. This was all so new to her, and she had no idea of what was going on! The noise of voices and bleeping was beginning to drown out as she closed her eyes to adjust to the brightness.

It panicked Richard for a few moments until he realised she was okay. It was a routine reaction from a patient in this condition. The signs were good, and at least this patient would have a life worth living again. For the doctors and nurses, it was a reward to see a comatose patient wake up and come alive unexpectedly. Stephanie didn't open her eyes again for a few minutes after that. It was a lot to cope with. Richard just starred at her, smiling, but he wasn't quite sure if she'd recognised him, as she hadn't spoken yet. It all took time and a lot of patience to wait until she was ready to say or do something. It was so frustrating, but everyone managed to stay calm. The boys didn't quite know what was happening, whether it was good or not. No one had had the time to explain it all to them. They really didn't know their mummy was waking up!

'Stephanie, can you hear me, darling?' the words were gentle and loving. They were words of which Richard showed his expression of love to Stephanie. Then silence fell all around as they waited and waited.

Her eyes slowly opened and blinked. She was staring back at him. 'Hi, honey!' Short but sweet, Stephanie gave them what they wanted to hear. She could speak and she recognised him instantly.

At that moment Callum leaped onto her bed and clung around his mother's shoulders as if he were frightened to let go, in case she were to disappear! But it was so loving and tender that it brought a tear to her eyes. She was okay but still wasn't aware of how she came to be in hospital. Richard slowly eased their youngest son, Jack, onto the bed and sat next to him. Jack squealed for his mummy and reached out for her instantly.

Stephanie was so overwhelmed to see her sons, she let out a little whimper. It was a relief to see such a reaction. It seemed as though things might be all right at last! All four of them just hugged one another for what seemed like eternity. Dr Rosenstein moved towards the bed and asked Stephanie if she felt okay; she nodded and looked friendly and rather happy.

'Can I talk to you for a moment alone, maybe, Mrs Sandlers?' he asked politely.

'Yes, you may, Doctor.'

He then turned to Richard. 'Would you mind, just for a few moments, if I spoke to your wife, Mr Sandlers?'

'Of course not,' Richard replied, and gathered the boys in his arms and left the cubicle to let the doctor look over Stephanie and maybe run a few tests. Callum was full of joy and laughter after seeing Stephanie. Jack put up a slight struggle as he wondered where his mummy had gone, but after a cuddle and a different view to look at he soon settled down. They sat further down the room near a window and Jack lay in his father's arms sucking on his bottle.

It was beginning to rain outside and Callum sat watching people outside trying to dodge the raindrops. He always looked like one of those children with the rain mac on and with the hat to match in a sunshine yellow colour. Probably a childhood memory of Richard's!

One of the nurses came over to Richard with a light refreshment of a drink of tea and orange squash for Callum. The staff were very kind and considerate, which made you appreciate the hard work they did. And it also made you feel lucky to be cared for by them in this hospital. Richard thought to ring Frances and tell her about Stephanie waking up. She would want to be there with them all. He wasn't allowed to use the phone in the ICU, as it was for hospital use only, but he was told there was a payphone down the corridor. By the time Jack had finished his bottle, Richard decided to go and make the call. It wasn't the best way to tell his mother-in-law, but even more so it could have been more of a shock if she had just turned up and just saw Stephanie awake and no one had told her! So Richard found a phone and called her quickly. It was a little time before she had managed to get to the phone; she'd just got out of the shower and she rushed to answer it.

'Hello?'

'It's Richard. Do you want some good news?' Richard sounded excited.

'What is it? Is Stephanie all right?' She hesitated.

'Yes, she's all right. She's awake, Frances, your daughter has come out of the coma.'

There was silence for a moment, followed by a bubbly cry of tears and laughter. She was awake and well. Frances became overwhelmed and tried to speak to Richard. 'Oh, my, I can't believe it! Can I see her?' She calmed down a little now. The tears were still rolling down her cheeks, soaking into her bathrobe. Her hair wringing wet as she sat on the bottom of her bed.

'When you're ready, I'm sure Stephanie would love to see you. She's seen the boys and held them.'

'Well, as soon as I'm dressed and calmed down, I'll get myself over there. Thanks, Richard, see you soon.'

And then Frances put the phone down and sat and cried to herself some more. After a while she composed herself enough to get dressed.

Richard left the phone and walked back to ICU, where his wife lay awake. The ward was buzzing with excitement and people were so cheerful. There were still more tests to do and checks and scans. It was early afternoon by the time Frances arrived at the hospital. She dressed very casually in jeans and a sweater, but she still looked good for her age. She was a fashionable gran, as Richard liked to think of her. None of the grey-haired, pleated skirt business, more of the sneakers and jeans lady. There she stood in the middle of the ward, staring at the bed her daughter was in, only the curtain had been pulled around the bed for the patients' privacy.

Richard came out from behind the curtains and greeted his anxious mother-in-law. She was still staring when he approached her. She seemed startled, and gazed into Richard's eyes, almost frightened of what she might see. They slowly walked over to the bed where Stephanie lay and Richard pulled back the curtain to reveal a beautiful woman with a golden glow about her.

Frances hesitated and wondered if it would be the same woman lying there, that she'd always known. Had the coma made her a different person or was she the same loving daughter and the best mother to her children? It surprised Richard at how long it took Frances to sit by Stephanie; the hesitation lasted for seconds. But she put her arms around Stephanie and cried. It was a mother and daughter reunion they'd all been waiting for and Frances realised everything was going to be okay at last. As Frances pulled away from her daughter, there were more tears streaming down both their faces. It was a real emotional moment to remember as Stephanie gazed into her mothers' eyes and gently smiled.

'Hi there, sweetheart,' her mother said, slowly stroking the beautiful hair that donned her daughters face. The boys were clearly no longer distressed, as they had seen their mother and were happy now!

'Mom.' A whisper left Stephanie's lips. She hadn't spoken for two weeks and her voice was weak.

But her mother instantly broke down in tears again with joy, knowing Stephanie could speak again and recognise her.

Dr Rosenstein walked into the ward, moments after Stephanie spoke, and he checked her over and asked the nurses more questions and asked for results of tests done that morning. Time was passing and it was suggested that they go for a bite to eat before they decided to explain to Stephanie how come she'd got to being in the ICU at Medway. As of the time being, no one knew how much she remembered from that fateful afternoon! Neither Richard nor Frances was especially hungry, but they nibbled a sandwich and the boys were eating well. It had been a stressful day so far and it wasn't over yet. What if more information came out about the accident than Richard intended?

Chapter Four

But only Richard and the two police officers knew the exact truth behind it all. It could easily go wrong. He would have to be careful, he thought. After lunch Richard decided it would be best if Laura would look after the boys for a few hours again, to make sure they could explain things to Stephanie without any interruption. Laura didn't mind at all; she was delighted at the news of Stephanie's recovery. It was beginning to look good for them after all.

She came and picked the boys up and swapped the baby seats from his car to hers and she took them back home. It had been a long morning for them both and they needed a nap. Richard left the car park and met Frances in the lift going back up to the ward. Stephanie was now sitting up and looking quite alert. It was strange to begin with as everything looked new to her, and she was trying hard to work out what she was doing there and then she saw them. Her mother and husband came into the ward with big smiles and she was absolutely beaming with beauty. She recognised them and that was reassuring to her.

'Wow, look at you, honey, you look great. How are you feeling? Boy, have we missed you!'

'I don't know what I'm doing here, Richard!' She was a little insecure, and that was to be expected, but he wasn't prepared for these questions so quickly. She might learn the truth sooner, now!

Dr Rosenstein was called over and they all sat down next to Stephanie's bed and Richard held her hand softly in his. They all knew this would be difficult for all of them, but they had to go through with it; she wanted and needed to know why she was there.

'Stephanie, do you remember anything about a shopping trip at all lately?' Dr Rosenstein said.

She shook her head. It did not mean anything.

'What do you remember last?' He insisted on slowly releasing small quantities of information discreetly, so as not to panic her. But her mother and husband were there to comfort her if she got distressed. Her voice was still weak and she was still hooked to the IV and monitors. But she was so wide-awake and alert that now was the time to get the questions answered.

'I can see our car tip over on its side, then only darkness, but I can hear crying and voices!' She had no recognition of anything before the accident, only the fact that they crashed. Sometimes coma patients could block out significant memories of the time and places when they awoke. This was very normal to the medical staff. Experiencing painful memories could be easily blocked. Even though she recognised her family now, she couldn't recollect the turn of events surrounding the accident from the moment of impact. It was obvious they would have to explain what happened that afternoon, when everything was so perfect and happy. Stephanie just sat and listened as both the doctor and her husband went through all the details of the accident.

She was silent all the way through, which they didn't expect. They were waiting for a reaction but all they saw were tears falling upon her fair skin. 'My boys, my boys.' Stephanie broke her silence and began to ask for her sons.

Richard calmed her down, explaining they weren't hurt, and her best friend was caring for them again tonight. 'I'll bring them to see you again later, darling!' Richard, still holding her hand, reassured her, her sons were well and were having a nap now at home. 'Stephanie, your mother came as soon as she could get a flight out. She's been here at your bedside for the past two weeks, talking to you with me and waiting for you to wake up. And here you are, awake and well.'

It startled her to realise just how long she'd been lying there lifeless, motionless and speechless. But the stories and laughter brought her back. They weren't going to give up on her and the work paid off. Stephanie was one of the few lucky ones. It was medical knowledge that after many years in a comatose state, some patients didn't ever wake up, and the families were left with the painful decision of turning the life support machines off. Thankfully this would never happen to Stephanie Sandlers.

'Thanks for coming, Mom, I love you.' Stephanie and her

mother were very close; they were good friends as well as mother and daughter, and it showed.

'I love you too, Stephanie. I'd do anything for you; you're still my little girl, you know!' Frances would do anything, like she had said. Stephanie was so important and special to her, especially since Harry had gone. Their bond had become so much stronger after that. Harry had been gone for a while now and Stephanie and the children were all Frances really had left. It was a lovely life for her over in America, but she soon made up for it when she came to England for her visits, without which she'd be totally lost. Today was one of those special moments in which she was glad she and her daughter were close. Frances was here for her daughter and that's what mattered now.

Although Stephanie sensed a little sadness in the air, she didn't have the energy to tackle it at this particular time. Richard was calm and purely watched Stephanie's reactions for ages. She was beautiful and sophisticated, even in these circumstances.

'I'll bring the boys in later to see you, darling,' Richard said. They were being well cared for by Laura and he knew Stephanie would understand that, once he explained.

And she did, but for the rest of the afternoon she lay there waiting, watching the time go by anxiously. But Stephanie needed her rest and had to do as the doctors had told her. She was stable now and almost had full marks for recovery. They still weren't sure of her capabilities at that point, but it was looking really good anyhow. The clocks ticked by and, after a few hours relaxing, Stephanie began to make conversation. And while she was having a little chat with her mother, Richard could hear his children entering the ward. Jack and Callum had arrived to see their mother awake, and her usual self. It was a sight he wouldn't have missed for absolutely anything. She squeezed them so tightly that Jack was almost squirming in her arms. She was delighted and very much a devoted mother. She noticed a few changes in the boys; they'd grown and looked different in a few ways.

Callum still had that cheeky smile and Jack had the same gorgeous giggle that she adored. Richard began to think that he could actually pull this off without Stephanie ever finding out the real truth behind her accident. How could he keep his secret? Would she really understand, or was it fate that this had happened to him now? They were questions he would have to answer in his own time and in his own way. Maybe one day it would be discovered but for now he had to keep the truth locked away like a nasty nightmare! Only he knew the reason and for now it would have to stay that way. She looked so happy, they had always been happy. They were a family united and he wanted it to stay that way!

The curtain to her bedside moved, and Laura stuck her head around. She was amazed at what she saw, her best friend looked the perfect patient. Stephanie showed a huge smile as she saw her best friend standing at the foot of the bed.

'Boy, do you surprise people!' It was a fact, but as Laura looked at her, she felt an overwhelming emotion.

'You can't keep a good thing down for long!' replied Stephanie.

After that there were even more tears and laughter and cuddles for all. It was a celebration; much was talked about that afternoon. And before anyone noticed, Stephanie was beginning to get tired and needed a rest. Everyone left and went to the hospital's tea area for refreshment and left Stephanie in the very capable hands of Dr Rosenstein. All normal checks were carried out and she was left to doze on the monitors; she was still on the IV but she was being supervised constantly in case she relapsed!

She was still asleep when they all came back from the tearooms. She wasn't disturbed for the rest of their visit. Laura had arrived in her own car so, after the informal exchange of baby seats, everyone went home. It turned out to be a very eventful day and they all had happy thoughts of Stephanie. At least she was awake now and out of danger. The music and voices had paid off. It was true what people said after all. They might be asleep but they know you are there.

After a few days Stephanie was given discharge from intensive care and bid a fond farewell to all the staff, who had all been so caring. It had been a nice place to be and the nurses were so caring, she made sure they were well rewarded. Flowers arrived with chocolates for all the staff in ICU. It was a gesture she knew they would appreciate and would like!

Richard picked Stephanie up from the hospital and drove her home. It was eerie for him and unnerving as he slowly remembered the last time the two of them had been in a car together. But Stephanie hadn't realised until they reached the drive of their home. As she looked out of the windscreen she felt a little panicked but tried not to say anything or let it show. Between the two they both felt panic-stricken, but neither wanted the other to know. Silence fell upon them as Richard parked up and turned the engine off. It was time to reflect and think for a moment. Would life ever be the same again? Would Stephanie ever be the same?

Suddenly the front door opened and some extremely happy faces appeared from behind. She had come home, there was so much excitement, and Stephanie could feel it.

Richard walked around the front of the car and opened the passenger door for her. She felt a little shaky and had to steady herself as she removed herself from the passenger seat. He put his arm around her as if to reassure her he was still there and they both walked up to the front door, where a welcome party greeted them. It was just a few polite friends from the area and Laura and Frances and the boys. Nothing extremely big or too exciting. But still it was time to celebrate, the boys had helped Frances bake a fabulous cake that read WELCOME HOME MUMMY. And there were streamers and balloons everywhere she looked. She was home, and she liked what she saw.

Slowly and gently she began to touch little things like ornaments and trinkets. The boys laughed and giggled. It was truly a special party for all to enjoy. There were plenty of people who had waited to see Stephanie, though only immediate family were allowed in ICU, so they were invited along to greet her at home. Nothing had been changed, no one had moved anything and there was a definite buzz to the whole party!

It was exciting and she didn't seem at all fazed by the whole idea at all. She starred at some recent family photos on the wall and smiled to herself as she remembered the day they were taken. I'm home, she thought to herself.

Richard took a back seat and carefully watched his wife swan around their home and soak up the atmosphere. There was laughter in the air and everyone was having fun. The boys seemed to get a lot of attention, too. Frances carried Jack around, to the delight of everyone. Callum wandered around and began to take interest in a particular toy on the floor, but he was enjoying himself and that was what really mattered.

After a while Richard strolled over to the friends Stephanie was with and gently held her hand and began to walk into the dining room, where there was the most wonderful cake on the table, just waiting to be eaten! It had been made between Jack, Callum and Frances and they couldn't wait any longer to present it to Stephanie. It was beautiful, and it said WELCOME HOME MUMMY. Everybody crowded around and Richard said a few words to welcome Stephanie back and they all raised their glasses as Stephanie looked totally amazed. Tears filled her eyes as she tried to speak. She hadn't seen a more beautiful cake, and it was truly special.

It was all too much for her; as she began to cry she almost fainted. Richard gently sat her on a dining chair and calmed her down. Everyone instantly realised it was too much to expect of her, and realised she must have been so overwhelmed that the entire afternoon became tiring!

'I'll be fine, really. I'm just still recovering.' She said it with style and dignity. She hadn't wanted her friends and family to feel unwanted. Just that it had been a long day and she needed time to herself. As the welcome party began to disband, Stephanie felt a huge amount of warmth from them and concern. But it was fantastic to have a welcome home party. It was a very kind gesture and a surprise. Friends left on the understanding that Stephanie was fine, just tired. And all gave her a loving hug and warm wishes. It was good for her to see them all again.

As the door closed, Stephanie felt faint again and beckoned Richard. It was time for a little rest upstairs. Frances was cleaning up after the visitors left, and Laura offered quietly to take the boys to the park for a walk. Richard accepted all the help offered and decided to take Stephanie upstairs for a lie down on their bed for a while. Richard wasn't at all surprised by how overwhelmed Stephanie had become. But at the same time he realised the whole afternoon was beginning to make him feel guilty again. Was this charade for his benefit or to keep Stephanie sweet without any suspicions?

Once he'd laid her on the bed and she'd closed her eyes, he walked over to the bedroom window and watched his wife's best friend leave the front drive with both his children, for a late afternoon stroll in the park. It made him think what he would do if the truth ever emerged. It would shatter their world entirely. Surely Stephanie wouldn't understand what really happened between him and 'the other woman'. After all, Stephanie had been expecting their second child at the time. And aren't husbands meant to be supportive to their expectant wives, not cheat on them?

Richard knew he would have to be very careful when questions arose around the accident. The door slightly ajar, Richard heard footsteps and as he turned from the bedroom window he saw Frances peeping around the door to look in on her daughter.

Stephanie was sleeping soundly and Frances smiled gently. It pleased her to see her beloved daughter resting when she most needed to. And she knew Stephanie was very well cared for. Richard starred at Frances and searched her eyes for any clues, in case she knew anything untoward had happened. But she had no idea; she thought it was all so innocent. They both stood side by side and watched Stephanie sleep.

'She's all I have apart from you and the boys,' Frances said. It was a lonely woman who said such words and sometimes it showed but Stephanie hadn't noticed. But she felt her home was in the States now, not England. She had many friends, but Harry was over there too. Frances had made her home over there, even though somehow she still felt lonely deep down in her heart.

Frances had been in constant touch with her friends over in the States to keep them in touch with Stephanie's progress; they were much relieved to hear of her recovery. But it reassured Frances to know all were concerned and they were there for her if she needed them. She felt so needed here now with Stephanie; here, she knew she could stay for as long as she wanted to. It was good to be here, and belong once more. Since moving to the States with Harry, only Stephanie was her last real connection to the homeland she once grew up in.

Stephanie lay there with little movement as she slept undisturbed; her right arm seemed to give her difficulty sometimes, as it was still in plaster, but once settled it hardly bothered her, although the plaster wouldn't be removed for another four weeks or so. It was hard to believe it was only two weeks ago that the whole nightmare had begun. A month was so far away, but they weren't really worried about it at all. Richard stood listening to his mother-in-law who was glad he was there to listen to her, and be there for her.

They both left the room to let Stephanie sleep a while. It had been a long day and everyone was exhausted. But it was good to have her home again. Two weeks ago, this day wasn't even considered at that moment, due to her condition! As the two of them came to the top of the stairs, they could hear a little song being sung; it was Laura and the boys. They had returned from the park in a very happy mood.

Richard opened the door to find Laura singing a song with Callum and Jack was in his pushchair, almost asleep. They had rosy-red cheeks and the wind had blown Laura's hair around, which Richard noticed and he giggled.

'May I ask what's so funny?' she inquired.

'You should see your hair; it suites you.' He just couldn't help himself and, as they all came in from the obviously windy weather, Richard directed her to the hall mirror and she too seemed to see the funny side. It was a mess but it was funny too.

Frances began to help Callum out of his coat and took him for a drink in the kitchen. Richard saw Jack was tired and decided to put him to bed. He didn't seem to mind about going to bed and nodded off as Richard undressed him and placed him in his cot.

After all the excitement calmed down, everyone sat in the kitchen to have a drink and a chat. Frances sat making polite conversation with her grandson while Laura and Richard talked about Stephanie and the party. She inquired on how Stephanie had been while they were in the park. Shortly after that, Laura had to leave as she had some errands to run and was watching the time, so she said her goodbyes and promptly left the house around 4 p.m. She knew she left later than expected but then Laura allowed herself to be late once in a while, as she never could tell just how her days would go!

A few days went past before she managed to call Stephanie and have a quick chat about how things were going. Stephanie enjoyed their chats. By the time normality set back in and routine was almost back to normal, it was time for Stephanie to have the plaster on her right arm removed. It was a great relief as she hadn't been able to do much with it out of action for so long.

While in the hospital she had a quick visit from Dr Rosenstein and he was so pleased with her progress. This sophisticated man behind the white doctor's coat intrigued her. She enjoyed their conversation and thanked him once again for all his help and encouragement.

It had been six weeks now since the accident and Frances began to notice things were going really well; maybe it was time to go home! Her daughter was recovered totally now and she felt a little homesick. So, one afternoon when they were all in the lounge watching the boys playing, Frances decided to bring the subject up and it seemed the right time to mention it. 'Darling, I know you're well again and everything is back to normal, the way it should be. I was thinking about heading home, soon.' She said it with such sadness.

'Oh. Mom, I'm so grateful for all your support through all of this. Of course I don't mind if you decide to go home now. You've given me so much of your time, I understand, really.' Tears welled in her eyes as they looked at one another and both of them hugged each other but didn't want to let go.

It was an emotional day, as Frances had decided to go home when she had made the appropriate arrangements. Stephanie and her mother decided that they would go out for the afternoon the next day and treat themselves to a mother and daughter afternoon. Richard would be home from work and he was going to watch the boys. It was certainly going to be lots of fun.

The next day soon came and both women were very excited about their little trip. The boys were being extremely good and behaving very well. Lunchtime was somewhat difficult as Callum couldn't decide what he wanted to eat; Jack was demanding his bottle at the same time and Richard wasn't due home for another two hours. But they managed to overcome the problem and Frances offered to feed Jack while Stephanie prepared Callum's lunch. They were both going to dine out somewhere special that lunchtime.

They took it in turn to get ready while the other watched the boys. Jack was placed in his playpen after his lunch as he was full of life. And Callum sat next to him to look at a few of his favourite books and play with the odd toy! They were both content and played happily.

Richard came home to find his two favourite ladies dressed to hit the shops. His lunch was in the fridge and he was hungry. He expressed his content by reassuring them both to have a good time. After all, what Stephanie needed most was normality. And he was going to make sure she was going to get it, even if it meant he would have to suffer with his guilt just that little bit more!

He had to hide his guilt so that absolutely no one had any idea. Which was probably the best thing all around as it would be a disaster. But for now things were going just the way he planned. Both Stephanie and her mother said goodbye and promised to be home later. So they left, only they didn't go as far as Stephanie's last trip took her! They went a lot closer to home and Stephanie began to show her feelings with her mother, and Frances began to listen and realise just how close they had all come to losing her and how frightened Stephanie had become at the thought of how one incident can do that to you, and how it can really put your life into perspective.

And it was a confusing time for Stephanie as she began to explain her fears and dreams to her mother; she wasn't quite sure what was really reality and what wasn't. 'You can tell a lot about a person if they hold any fear, Mom, yet I really don't know if anyone can see it in me.' Stephanie said it so boldly it startled her mother for a moment.

'But I wasn't aware you were feeling like this inside, darling.'

But did Frances really know her daughter that well, if she could not see the fear? The subject got so intense at one point that they dared not carry on the conversation, in case one of them backed out on their emotions at the last minute. Stephanie had never felt this way before and now Frances could see she was hurting inside.

'I suppose I'm probably just frightened or scared about my feelings about what happened to me! Richard wants to assure me that I am really okay and that our life is so normal again, but I'm not sure.'

'Well, if you do feel differently about anything, you should tell your husband and try to solve the problem before it does any damage,' Frances insisted.

'But that's just it. Richard hasn't really talked about that dreadful day, hardly at all. I want him to know my feelings and how confused I feel right now. Does he really know me, Mom?'

That afternoon was supposed to be fun-filled and full of laughs and catching up on things between mother and daughter. Instead, there they were discussing the inner most feelings one could ever have. But Frances really needed to know and listen to what her daughter was trying to tell her. The question was, did Frances have the answers for her? She herself didn't think she was the right one to advise and give help, but she was going to try.

'Maybe I should spend a little time with Richard when we get home and get to the bottom of this problem as soon as I can.'

Stephanie looked to her mother for support and found herself having one of the most wonderful cuddles a mother and daughter could ever share.

'I'm so glad I'm here to help you, sweetheart. I want you to know I'm here if you should ever need me. And don't let a silly little thing like the Atlantic Ocean ever put you off!'

It was a funny thing to say but it put a smile on Stephanie's face. They needed each other so much and today was a really good day to express that need. The two decided to shop and have lunch in a quiet little teashop and Frances was thrilled as it was so different to their busy diners back home!

It proved to be a successful day. Many questions were unanswered, but Stephanie certainly felt much better. It was good to get out for a while and routine was beginning to take shape again, as Richard had been back at work a week or so by then, and even he looked revived when he came home at the end of the day.

'What do you say we go and treat ourselves, Stephanie, and really go to town? I could do with a new outfit for a friend's birthday bash next month. What do you say?'

'Well, I'm up for it if you are, Mum.' Stephanie's face lit up as Frances promised they would have a good time.

They left the teashop and hit the shops big time, trying on fancy hats and accessories. And the jewellery store was showing some great taste in the display window. Stephanie bought herself a twenty-two-carat gold choker. She enjoyed fancy jewellery like that and, much to her amazement, noticed her mother wasn't holding back on her pocket change herself. She didn't seem to care how much her earrings and bracelet were. But what the hell, they were enjoying themselves, and what's more they'd been told to treat themselves as it was Richard who'd funded the trip.

They went on to buy fantastic outfits and of course the shoes and bags to match. Stephanie wasn't quite sure when she would get to wear her new choice of clothes but it was fun buying them. She'd put on a few extra pounds since the accident, but that didn't bother her; it gave a new shape to her almost perfect figure. Frances had definitely enjoyed every minute of their day together.

As they made their way home, there was an unnerving silence in the air. Stephanie looked grey in the face and Frances realised how her daughter must have been feeling. It became all too clear Stephanie was beginning to remember the horrors of her accident. Nothing was said all the way home; it put a dampener on the afternoon, to say the least. As Stephanie's home came into view, she turned to her mother and tears fell on her face and the pain spoke for itself. She couldn't believe how close they'd come to loosing their lives on that fateful day.

But now was what mattered and when they both tried to speak, a muffled cry was all that could be heard. It became so real, so soon. After unloading the car, they stopped for a moment and hugged each other. It said it all, a few kind words of encouragement, a hug and a smile. That was what mothers were for. And Stephanie certainly needed her mother right then!

'Don't forget, you need to have a few words with Richard and let him know just how you're feeling, otherwise he can't help you.'

'Okay, Mom,' said Stephanie, as if she were being scolded like a child done wrong!

Chapter Five

Stephanie reached into her bag for her house keys. As they both walked into the house Callum came running and hugged them both. Jack was in his playpen. Frances took her bags upstairs and gave Stephanie some time with Richard while she looked over her new clothes.

'Where's Daddy, Callum?'

'Daddy's talking on the telephone, Mummy,' Callum replied.

So, holding onto her son's tiny hand, she slowly walked into the lounge to see Richard with his back turned to her, as she came through the door. But he hadn't seen her arrive home, either!

'I don't care, Michaela, you shouldn't have been there. This is your entire fault. My wife could have died, not forgetting my two sons. Do you have any idea what you have done to my family?' Richard obviously had no idea he was being watched or listened to. The phone call had happened at completely the wrong time. But there was no turning back now.

Stephanie stood in amazement at what she had just heard. How could this be? Who was her husband talking to? Callum tried to let go of his mother's hand to let his father know she was home, but Stephanie just held on to him and as he looked up he saw his mother crying. Stephanie bent down to speak to Callum; with her face soaked in tears she gently whispered to him to go upstairs and tell granny he was to stay with her. Off he went upstairs, while his dad had no idea Stephanie could hear every word he was saying. Then, without any warning, Stephanie banged the lounge door; at that moment Richard turned around to see his beautiful wife standing there behind him and she looked devastated.

'Oh my god, Stephanie, how long have you been standing there?'

'Long enough to hear every word you have been saying to another woman.'

They both stood there in disbelief, at what had just happened. Their world was slowly being pulled in every direction.

'What the hell is going on, Richard?' Stephanie's tears dried up and she felt anger instead of grief. She wasn't going to let it go until she found out what had been going on.

At that point, a voice came through the phone; Richard realised he was still holding the phone in his hand and he just stood there staring at it, and listened to the woman on the other end!

'Hello, Richard, are you still there? Speak to me, damn it!' She was getting annoyed.

'Eh, eh, I'll have to call you back. It's not a good time to talk right now.'

Hesitating, Richard put the phone down and looked at his wife. Still in disbelief, he began to shake his head and mumble something to himself. But what was more irritating was that he wasn't even trying to explain what this was all about. He just stood there while their perfect world began to crumble right before his very eyes.

Stephanie was standing there when her body began to shake and she felt dizzy. Suddenly she had collapsed into a heap on the floor and it was Richard who cried out to her. Richard, holding her in his arms, crying, was the scene that his mother-in-law first saw when she came down to see what was going on. It was frightening, as she hadn't known what had been said downstairs. It occurred to her that maybe Stephanie had had a relapse, but this wasn't the case. She had fainted and it looked worse than it actually was!

'Stephanie, darling, can you hear me? What happened, Richard?'

Richard just looked through his watery eyes and only said 'Sorry,' over and over again, which only puzzled Frances even more as she still didn't know what was going on.

Suddenly Stephanie began to stir and move, and when she opened her eyes and saw Richard holding her she let out such a cry it shook him! 'Get away from me, Richard. I don't want you near me. Just get away.' She sobbed until Richard got up from her side and moved into a corner of the room like a naughty child.

He didn't know what to do next, so he just stood there and

watched as his wife gained her composure and moved from the floor to the nearest chair, aided by her mother.

'Now, are you going to tell me what on earth is going on or what?' she scolded intensely.

Richard couldn't turn back now. He would have to tell his dirty little secret after all. He hadn't wanted his mother-in-law to know it so soon or in this way, but it didn't look as if she was going to leave the room, until she knew what was going on!

'Richard, I think you should tell us both what exactly it is you have done – and I want the truth and all of it!' Stephanie already felt weak, but also the hurt inside was so dreadful she thought her heart was broken. He had betrayed her and that was so devastating and so obvious by what she heard on the phone that there could be no mistake.

'Mom, I think you should sit down. I'm sure Jack will be fine playing in the playpen and Callum's next to it with some toys. Richard is going to tell us both everything.'

'It's very simple, Stephanie. I made a very big mistake and I regret it but I fear it may be too late now!' He began to sweat as the pressure was mounting. And his wife wanted an explanation. 'I had a brief affair when you were pregnant with Jack and it just went too far. I was never going to leave you, Stephanie. It all happened so quickly. God knows, the guilt I've been carrying around with me all this time. I never thought anything would ever happen like this!'

'What do you mean, like this?' Frances asked very nervously.

'While I was getting incredibly fat and frumpy, he obviously decided to sleep with someone else, some one more attractive than his wife, and she must have been very pretty too! I can't believe it happened. Now what are you going to do about it?' Stephanie remarked.

Frances wanted to keep her composure while the discussion was taking place so she didn't say too much.

The room fell silent. Not a word was said and Stephanie sat with tears rolling down her cheeks and her mother comforting the broken daughter by her side. The truth seemed so dirty now. Stephanie couldn't bear to look at her husband! Her world was just beginning to recover and mend itself when this awful abrupt moment destroyed everything.

Was this how life was meant to be? Hurting one another until there was no feeling left at all? Was she meant to say anything to defend him, or was she supposed to slap his face and call him awful names? Her head felt so confused and she was hurt by it all. She had had no idea anything had been going on at all behind her back.

'How long have you been seeing this woman?' Stephanie asked, trying to calm herself.

'You were in your second trimester when we first started seeing one another. It was very casual but discreet. I stopped seeing her when you had Jack. It wasn't at all serious. I didn't see her again, but I was horrified to hear she was in the other car, as I didn't take any notice of who was at the hospital or anything.'

'Did she cause the accident, Richard? Did you know what really happened?' inquired Frances.

'I told you, I stopped seeing her, it must have been a coincidence for her to be at the shops too. But I didn't see this woman when you did. And I can't say whether or not she recognised me and followed us home.'

It was as plain as the nose on her face that the woman had seen them together, got jealous and decided to take revenge on the man she loved. Only it had gone too far, this time, she had endangered the lives of a whole family and Richard's wife had been left in a coma.

But there was nothing now that could change this. It was the horrible truth and now they all knew.

'So why wait until now to let me find out? Were you ever going to tell me what you had done?' she said.

'You came home when I least expected you, Stephanie. I was trying to resolve the whole situation without hurting anyone. But now it's backfired and everyone has been hurt. I just don't know what to do or say to you. None of this was ever meant to happen, but it did, and I'm truly sorry, honest I am. I love you. You mean so much to me but I made a terrible mistake. I'm so sorry!'

The words 'I'm sorry' didn't mean anything to her now. She had been hurt mentally and physically and no one could feel the pain as much as she did at that moment. Because of this stupid mistake, she had been in a coma, and her arm had been broken. She could have died. And her children had been traumatised by the whole experience. Is that what this woman had really intended to do, kill Richard or his family?

Even Richard didn't know the answer to that one.

'Was she hurt at all, just to see who came off worse, or was I the only injured party in all this?'

Stephanie didn't really want to know but she was so curious. But anything else really wasn't worth knowing.

'I haven't really asked. I was trying to find out how this happened and why she was there,' he said.

'Well, I think I know everything I need to know. Now I'm going out for a while. Mom, could you watch the boys for me? I just need to be by myself right now.'

Stephanie left the room as Richard tried to speak, but she ignored him. He had hurt her and she hated him for it. What would she do now? How could she live with a man who couldn't stay faithful and always had someone else on the side? She felt used and unwanted. Why hadn't he told her before? If they were so happy together, why would he lie to her and destroy everything they had?

She left the house as silently as she had entered and tears were raining down her face. She wanted to get out of the house and be alone for a while. She felt and looked awful but she didn't care. Everything was crammed into such a small amount of time that it was only sinking in now and she had to try to think reasonably.

But she had her mother with her at home and that was a lot of comfort to her right now. Time was getting on and Stephanie felt she had been walking for hours. She arrived back home somewhat more composed and calmer. She had figured out in her heart what the best solution was and now she had to explain it to her family!

Stephanie opened the door and Callum greeted her with a warm hug and kisses. Frances came from the lounge, holding Jack, and asked if she was all right. But after a few awkward moments the whole family went and sat around the dining table and tried to be as normal as possible for the boys' sake. But it wasn't at all easy, as it was quiet and Stephanie looked miserable even though she tried her hardest not to be.

Frances had prepared an evening meal while Stephanie had been out, and tried to keep things as they should be. The conversation was minimal at the meal table that evening, and as the two innocent faces glared at their parents it had become apparent that they knew something was wrong.

But Callum didn't mention anything until it was time to go to bed. Stephanie let them say goodnight to Richard and Frances, then took them upstairs to bath them and read them a bedtime tale.

'Are you upset, Mummy?' By the look on his face, he saw the pain his mother was in and wanted to help her!

'Oh, my darling, I'll be okay, you'll see,' she said with such sincerity. The situation became difficult, as now Stephanie had realised that her sons had detected the unhappiness between them both.

As she ran a bubbly bath for Jack first, she laid him on the baby-changing unit, and watched him kick his little feet about and gurgling away to himself. She often found herself watching her sons and wondering just what they were thinking. As Stephanie began to undress Jack, she felt the presence of someone watching her as she slowly turned, tears welled in her eyes and she had to turn away so he didn't see her cry.

Richard immediately went to put his hand on her shoulder but she saw and asked him to leave as quietly as he could. Callum touched her hand instead as he looked at his mother in a pool of tears once again, for the third time that afternoon, much to his bewilderment. What was it all about?

Slowly Stephanie eased Jack into the bath of bubbles; the cute little face of this young baby was wonderful.

How could Richard do this to her when she was carrying their second child? Didn't their marriage mean anything? If not, why had she had another baby with him? The questions were getting harder and harder to answer now and she had no help with any of it. How many more fateful blows was she to endure at this terrible time in her life?

Both boys laughed as Jack splashed and kicked his little legs in the bubbles. They dearly loved each other and she could see it clearly now. As Jack's time in the bath ended Callum began to undress himself to get into the lovely bubbly bath. Stephanie dried Jack and laid him back on the changing unit, and tended to Callum blowing bubbles in the air. Bath time was always fun, no matter how they were all feeling.

When Callum began to get tired, she dressed them both for bed, and as she placed each one into bed she felt as though she was going to cry again, but held it off so not to upset them both. When they were safely tucked up in their beds, she began to concentrate on what she would say when she went downstairs. It was going to be a long night!

Feeling tired and stressed out, Stephanie came down the stairs and saw the two solemn faces at the kitchen table, awaiting the inevitable conversation to erupt.

Frances got up from her seat and walked over to her weary-looking daughter. 'Is there anything I can do, Stephanie?' she asked quietly.

'No, Mom, I just need to sit with you both and tell you how I feel. You need to hear what I have to say.' Stephanie stayed calm. 'I have had a lot of time to think things over, and now I know I have to discuss it with you both.'

It was a solid statement. The whole idea of informing them both that she had future plans and what her future held for her wasn't going to be easy to explain. But Stephanie couldn't see any other option as her trust in her husband had totally disappeared into thin air, and with it her self-esteem and confidence. Life was going to throw everything it had in her path. She would have to cope alone now and face new challenges. There were possibilities that lay ahead that she would have to face.

As Stephanie stood in the doorway, she asked her mother and husband to follow her into the lounge. Richard didn't know what to expect from Stephanie at this point, as he wasn't sure what she was thinking any more. It worried him, as this situation had never occurred before. As Richard walked behind Frances, he gently shut the door and sat in the far end of the lounge, waiting nervously. Stephanie just waited calmly for a few minutes until she was ready to begin her explanation about what she had decided to do.

'These past few hours have been very painful and difficult, and I want you to know what I am about to tell you both is not easy for me to say. I want you both to listen to what I have to say, because it's for the best and I will not change my mind.'

She looked so serious and solemn, it broke her mother's heart. 'Stephanie, I hope you aren't going to do anything irrational!'

Richard, became frightened now, as Stephanie had clearly decided to stick to the decision she had made.

'Richard, please listen to me. I'm very hurt at the minute and I could be doing without this right now, talking to you! I don't want to be here with you any more, Richard. It's because of you and that woman I was left in a coma for two weeks. I don't even know if I'll ever get over it. I'm leaving you Richard, I've made the decision to fly out to America with Mom and stay with her for a while. I know it's a big step to take but that's the way I want it.' Stephanie sat there staring at the shocked look on Richard's face and look of surprise on her mother's face. Neither of them was expecting to hear such a shocking statement!

'You hate me that much, you want to move to the other side of the world to get away from me?' Richard felt so distressed at her decision, he began to sob and held his head in his hands. He knew he must have destroyed her to make her do such an awful thing. But now he would have to live with what he had done to his beautiful wife. Her hair glowing in the lamplight's shadow, she was more beautiful than the day they first met. Yet he'd managed to completely destroy what they both had in a matter of days. How could he have been so stupid? What was he thinking?

'Richard, you have to understand, you have taken away my most precious possessions, my trust in you and my respect for you. Surely you can't imagine I'd forgive you at the drop of a hat, all because you made a mistake? No, I don't hate you; I hate the fact you have made a fool of me and what you have done to me!'

'Stephanie, you're my daughter and I'll do anything to help you if you let me. And if you want to come back with me, then that is fine with me. Just please get this whole unfortunate mess cleared up, first, so you both know where you stand with each other.' Frances made herself quite clear and didn't say any more.

'I want to take the boys with me, Richard. I hope you will

agree with this decision and not make it difficult for me,' she said.

'You want to fly to America with our children, without me, and not expect me to make any noise over it? Well, I'm sorry but I think you must be stupid. I will not let you take both our sons away from me for the rest of their lives. I know now you will not be coming back to England, if you take both boys!' Richard felt angry and wasn't going to let her do it.

Stephanie didn't intend to make him angry, but she thought she was doing what she thought was right.

She had never done anything selfish in her life before now, but this was her children's future she was thinking about. So what was going to happen now? There was a big question mark over the rest of this supposedly civilised conversation. It was plain to see Richard wasn't going to let this happen without a fight! There was no one now to side with Richard; he was on his own. But he wasn't going to let this get in the way of his judgement of the whole situation. It was so easy to tell Stephanie what he would do to her and what he wouldn't! It was clearly the boy's interest they were both looking at. The decision had to be considered very carefully, and not to be taken lightly. The damage had been done and it was irreversible, and there was nothing Richard could do about it.

'What will you do in the States?' Richard remarked seriously.

'I'm not without my career, you know. I will be able to pick up my life and start a new one, maybe my own line in fashion. Who knows what I'm capable of Richard? I could be even more qualified in America.' Stephanie wanted him to know she wasn't intending on being the one who needed a man in her life to succeed. And that she plainly indicated to Richard.

Frances left the room discreetly, to let them have some time privately to talk things through. The boys needed her to keep an eye on them while all this mess was being sorted out. She went upstairs to find that Callum had heard the raised voices, and had gone to the top of the stairs to see what was going on. He hadn't heard much because the lounge door was shut, but he knew there was something wrong all the same.

'Hello, there, what are you doing out of bed, sweetheart?' Frances wasn't quite sure what to say to her darling grandson.

'I want Mummy.' Callum was almost half asleep as he spoke to Frances.

'I'm sure when Mummy has finished talking to Daddy she will come and tuck you in and give you a special bedtime cuddle.' Frances then picked Callum up and gently placed him back in his own little bed, and kissed him on the forehead as she pulled his bedding over him.

He had closed his eyes even before she reached the bedroom door. Frances then decided to check on Jack as maybe he could have woken too by the activity going on in the lounge. But as she peered around the door of his nursery, he was soundly sleeping with his tiny hands clutching a little teddy bear. The boys were all right, so Frances went to her own room for a short while to sit and come to terms with her daughter's future and what life might hold for them all now.

Frances analysed the situation for a while and thought to herself how things had made such a dramatic turnaround. Richard would undoubtedly have to consider his moves thoroughly as, if his wife did decide to leave him, he would still have to work and maybe still keep the family home, but through all this how would he cope with the children? Surely Stephanie wouldn't leave both boys behind. It wasn't something about which Frances yet really knew the outcome! But she did know that Richard didn't really have anyone to fall back on, unlike his wife who had her mother by her side.

Richard was a loner, whose parents had long since passed away. He had no immediate family he could turn to; it was him, and him alone in the world, all against the huge mistake he had made. Frances just couldn't understand why he had done such a stupid thing, and put everything he had ever worked for at risk. But it was the back seat she would have to take on this occasion and wait for the outcome like anyone else.

The phone rang in the hall, and Frances came downstairs to answer it, so as not to disturb them in the lounge. It was Laura calling to find out how the shopping trip had gone.

Frances struggled to say something on the other end to her daughter's best friend. 'I really think you should speak to Stephanie rather than me, but I can tell you we had a lot of fun shopping. Anyway, how are you? And how's work?'

'Is there something I should know about Frances? You sound a little nervous.'

Laura was on to her; she hadn't meant to give anything away, but it was hard as Laura knew her so well. 'I'm sorry, but I really can't tell you. Stephanie is going to have to tell you herself, my dear, but please don't worry, I'll tell her to give you a call either later or tomorrow.'

'If you are sure that's what you want. I'll see you soon, and give the boys a big hug from me. Bye, Frances.'

'Goodnight, Laura, and thank you for calling.' Frances put the phone down and left the hall as quickly as she had arrived there!

It was around 11.35 p.m., when Stephanie finally emerged from the lounge, weary-eyed and very tearful. She was utterly exhausted and the strain on her face showed she had been through hell. She slowly began to climb the stairs and sighed to herself; it had been one of the longest and toughest nights of her life so far.

She reached the top of the stairs and walked into Callum's room to find his little night light still on and he lay there with such calm and peacefulness. She hesitated, not wanting to wake him, and gently kissed his angelic face, then left him to sleep. And in turn she crept quietly into Jack's room to check he was okay, repeated the same reassurance, the gentle kiss and left.

As Stephanie approached her mother in the guest room, the door opened and Stephanie was face-to-face with Frances. The look in her daughter's eyes was now empty; something had died inside her and it was so clear to see. From that moment on, Stephanie had a new mission in life: to look after her sons without a partner. That much she was capable of, surely.

'I'm so sorry, Mom, I don't know how I'll get through this, but I'll do it. I have found something out tonight. I don't need my life the way it is right now and I don't ever want to be hurt like this ever again by another human being.' And instantly she broke down in tears, as her mother took her into the guest room to comfort her.

It had been a very strange day all around, Richard returning to work, her confiding in her inner most sacred thoughts to her mother, and then returning home to find her husband had been having an affair while she had been carrying their second child!

It was so much to absorb in one whole single day. Just how much more was she expected to take? But it was late now and Stephanie stayed the rest of the evening in the guest room with her mother. Surely Richard wasn't expecting her to share the same bed as him for the rest of her time in the house? As Stephanie drifted off to sleep with her mother's arm around her, Frances heard footsteps outside the door, but then they faded away and she heard a bedroom door gently close.

Richard knew where he stood with his wife. It was as he had feared; their marriage had disintegrated within twenty-four hours, right before his very eyes!

Chapter Six

There was a loud banging at the door the next morning; it alarmed everyone in the house at such an early hour. No one was in a good mood to begin with. Richard ran down the stairs to open the door to a very angry man. At first he had no idea who the man could be, but after a lot of crude remarks he clearly realised who the man was. It was Michaela's very angry, very bitter husband, Lawrence Stornton.

Richard immediately told Stephanie to go back upstairs to the children, as he didn't want to let her see anything if things got out of hand.

Although he hadn't said who this person was, Stephanie had already figured it out anyway. It seemed as though she wasn't the only one to get hurt in all this; the other woman was also married. The whole situation had got out of control and it looked as if the man wasn't going to let Richard get away with what he had done.

'You've ruined my marriage, you idiot. Do you have any idea how happy we were until you came along?' he shouted at Richard.

It was a little while before Richard managed to get his view across to the angry man who stood before him. 'Let me tell you, we didn't intend for anyone to get hurt in all this confusion. We only had a brief affair. It ended quite some time ago now.' Richard had to shout to get himself heard.

The shouting was beginning to wake up the surrounding neighbours. The sleepy village didn't usually get this kind of attention. Richard decided to ask Lawrence to come indoors, but that proved to be a bad idea. As soon as Richard showed him into the lounge to try to calm him down, Lawrence thumped him right in the eye and then went in for the kill. It was an unprovoked attack, as Richard wasn't ready for it; neither was he the violent type! Richard regained his self-esteem and threw a punch back to try to knock him to the floor, as he had done to Richard. But Lawrence was a lot bigger than Richard, and things didn't look good at all.

By now Richard's face was beginning to swell up and turning a horrible purple colour, and his lip was doing the same, but he had to keep up with this brute before he could give himself proper attention. As Richard stood up to Lawrence once again, he was knocked straight to the ground again and this time he wasn't going to get back up to fight back. Lawrence wasn't going to be satisfied until he had done what he had to do, and that was to hurt Richard badly.

And that was exactly what happened. There was a lot of shouting going on. When Stephanie finally came down on her own, the brute had run out of the door, knowing that Richard would bring charges against him; Richard could barely move when Stephanie found him!

'Oh, my god, Richard, what did that monster do to you? Who was he?' She seemed concerned, but also knew it was no more than he deserved.

Stephanie ran into the hall and called a doctor to come out to Richard. There wasn't any problem as it was before surgery hours. Stephanie called to her mother, and told her not to bring the children downstairs at all for the time being! It was a confusing time all around as no one seemed to know what to say to each other.

The doctor arrived quickly and, while he was looking after Richard, Stephanie went upstairs with a drink and breakfast for her mother and the children. She asked her mother to keep the children occupied while their daddy got cleaned up a bit. It would be too distressing for them to see him in such a state. Richard had taken a severe beating from the other woman's husband, who obviously didn't care how bad the damage was as long as he got revenge on Richard!

The doctor didn't ask any questions regarding how Richard got into such a state, but he did indicate that Richard had sustained broken ribs that morning. He wrapped Richard in crepe bandages and told him to rest up for a few days, as there wasn't anything he could do for fractured or broken ribs. As for the black eye and busted lip, an ice pack would cure that and the swelling would eventually go down.

But now Richard's pride was hurt and it would be hard to explain it to anyone why he had taken such a beating. He wasn't the same handsome husband any more.

Stephanie came downstairs as the doctor was ready to leave. He quietly took her to one side and asked if they were all right.

'Thank you for your concern, Doctor, but this is a battle Richard will have to fight on his own. He has made a mess of his life and he will have to get over it. The beating he was given this morning was by his woman friend's husband, if you get my drift!' Stephanie was quite blunt with her words, but the doctor understood and left without further comment.

Richard didn't have a lot to say to Stephanie, apart from a polite thank you for calling the doctor. She helped him up the stairs and took him into the bedroom, where he would have to rest up for a while. After settling him down, she left the room to see her sons. They were just finishing their breakfast as she entered the bedroom. Jack was being fed his bottle by Frances and Callum sat on the floor drinking his morning beaker of tea! Frances asked if everything was all right now, but Stephanie just shook her head and looked extremely shaken by the experience of what she had just witnessed.

It was obvious now what she had to do. How could she stay in a relationship where she felt so let down and was treated as if she was stupid or didn't even know what was going on in her own marriage? The boys looked at their mother, who was barely holding it together. Stephanie had to be strong for the boys' sake; she couldn't let them down now, and she would have to get though this really difficult patch virtually on her own. Richard wouldn't be much help now, he was too busy licking his own wounds to worry about his family! His pride had been hurt and now he was hiding in his room, trying to block out the world.

There was much to organise as she wasn't going to hang about to wait for Richard to make amends. It seemed that now Richard was no longer going to battle to keep his wife, but he wasn't going to let her take both the children away to the States. Richard had a good reputation as a lawyer and knew the way that system worked. And with the right guidance through the right channels he would be able to put a block on Stephanie taking both the children out of the country. Or at least that was the intention, anyway.

Stephanie said it was okay to go downstairs and Frances picked up Jack and took him to the top of the stairs while Stephanie took Callum's hand, and they all came down the stairs to sit in the kitchen and, while the boys played quietly, they sat down to discuss what had happened that morning. Stephanie didn't know where to start, but when she explained who the man was, the look of disappointment became apparent on her mother's face. Frances wanted to shield her daughter from the terrible time she was having, but there was absolutely nothing she could do!

After a while Stephanie just burst into tears at the thought of her impending departure from a loveless marriage, one that she had always thought that would withstand absolutely anything that marriage threw at them! But sadly this wasn't the case, as she couldn't stand the deceit and torment of knowing that her husband had been with another woman, and that she hadn't even known it was happening. It was time to move on with her life, and start a new one elsewhere. Sure, it would be daunting to begin with, but she was sure it would work its way into a new beginning, for her and her sons.

Frances tried to help Stephanie by offering to help bring the boys up and give her all the support she needed and encouragement to make her start a new life. Stephanie's mind had definitely been made up and she was going to leave Richard as soon as possible. But now was the time to act and get things done while it was still fresh in her mind; she had to get in touch with a very good solicitor to get everything on the move.

Stephanie went upstairs to get the boys some clothes so she would be able to get her divorce on the move as soon as she could. It was important to let Richard know she was serious. She wasn't going to take pity on him because he'd taken a beating. As far as she was concerned, he deserved exactly what he'd got from that man.

It was Friday and Stephanie knew she had a lot to get done by the weekend. She noticed their bedroom door was slightly ajar. Stephanie slowly walked in to see Richard did look in a bad way, but that was only because she had never seen him like this before.

As she got near his bedside, Richard turned to face her, tears in his eyes; he didn't know where to begin. He felt so ashamed of what he had done to her. He had degraded her and humiliated her and he was sorry, but deep down he knew he would never be able to repair the damage he had done. How do you tell someone that you had done something so bad that you wanted to make the hurt and shame go away? It was impossible. There was no way Stephanie would ever forgive him, not now. He looked at her and once again saw the pain and he felt it too, only his pain was physical; Stephanie was in pain mentally. It was as clear as day that it was over; the marriage, the love they shared, everything was gone! The weekend went by so fast; then it was Monday again and routine took charge once more. A lot of things didn't mean anything to her now; an empty feeling took hold of her. Stephanie hadn't wanted the situation to get as bad as it had but this was what it had come to and there was absolutely nothing she could do about it. She didn't want to be around Richard any more. He'd changed; his attitude was different towards everything. She sensed that through all the hospital situation and her recovery he had been covering it all up, giving her all the love and caring she needed and deep down he had another woman. It was all making sense now; the guilty looks, the loss for words and so on.

Was it all lies? Stephanie was now wondering if Richard was intending to leave her and the children for this other woman. She didn't know him, how he felt or what he was thinking any more. Richard wasn't as bruised as much now and he was up and about, but tried to avoid any conversation on Michaela or much else for that matter. It was as if he had lost all hope of gaining what he had lost; he wasn't in any frame of mind to discuss any intimate details with his wife about their future whatsoever. Stephanie carried on with her arrangements and filed for a divorce with a very professional firm of solicitors. She was actually getting somewhere with everything else going on; the boys were really being good for her. She rarely left them in the care of their father, as Richard was totally in a world of his own, most times. Frances helped out quite a lot, and it was a huge relief to Stephanie as she could no longer count on her husband.

By the end of the week Richard had begun to stop feeling

sorry for himself and decided to go into the office. Stephanie stuck it out until Richard was willing to talk serious arrangements over the children. The very thought of it made Stephanie cringe as she knew she was in for a tough time trying to agree on arrangements. Richard's black eye and swollen lip, had almost gone and he felt he was up to talking politely to his wife, as he had been ignoring her for almost a week now which wasn't easy as they were both constantly around each other day and night!

Another week had passed, and now it was make or break time! The atmosphere was so tense that it was almost unbearable. Both Stephanie and Richard had to sit down and talk as they had never talked before. Laura hadn't contacted Stephanie all the time this had been going on and Stephanie felt it was for the best. But still Stephanie missed her best friend through all the turmoil that she was in.

When everyone else was out and the house was quiet, Richard asked Stephanie to sit in the lounge to talk openly about what to do. As the nervous couple sat in the lounge at opposite ends of the room, they were now estranged. It was a pitiful sight to see!

'I want to talk calmly here and try to come to some kind of civilised agreement about the children, Stephanie, but I will warn you I don't want you to take my sons away from me. I'm not a monster of any kind and I won't have you portraying me as one, either.'

All went silent as Stephanie listened to him; she had to keep her cool otherwise Richard could prevent her from doing what she wanted, and he wasn't without influence!

'I too wish to be civilised about this, Richard, but I'm their mother. They need me. It's the mother who is favoured in the court rather than the father. You've got to understand, I want to take them with me. I love them too dearly to put them through this misery of an unhappy home.'

'I can't let you take both, Stephanie.'

He wasn't going to move, he would do anything to keep Callum. There had not been any favouritism between either of the boys, but even so Richard didn't think Callum would want to leave his father.

'You don't mean I can only take one of my sons without the

other?'

She couldn't believe what he had said; he must be joking! 'I can't go to America and leave one of my sons behind, Richard!' Stephanie began to cry and shake her head; it was impossible for a mother to do something so unkind. But it wouldn't be Stephanie being unkind, it would be all Richard's fault. But Callum wouldn't understand that. It was so awful, what Richard expected of her. The atmosphere was horrendous, to say the least. They had both known that this moment would arrive at some point, although the situation was almost at breaking point.

Stephanie was in shock at what her husband expected her to do. She couldn't imagine the thought of leaving one of her sons behind. Surely he wasn't thinking straight. He must have taken such a bad beating that it had knocked his common sense, as it was really unreasonable of him to make such demands. 'I'm sorry, Richard, you must be out of your mind. No way will I leave one of my children behind with you, so you can have one of your other women to look after him!' Stephanie was beginning to feel a lot angrier by now and she wasn't afraid to show it.

'You'll have no choice if I get a court order forbidding you to leave the country with both my sons.' He was being cruel with his words now, and he didn't care if he hurt her more than need be! 'You know how powerful I can be in the system, Stephanie. You simply can't think I'll let you get away with it. You'll have the fight of your life if you think you can take me on!'

She was aware that it was possible for him her husband to make her life a living misery. But now the tables had been turned; Richard was going to make it look as if Stephanie was the one who couldn't look after the children. She knew what he was up to and she wasn't going to be made the scapegoat to get him out of a really bad situation.

'You play it your way, Richard, and I'll play it my way. May the best person win, if that's the way you want it done.' Stephanie walked out of the lounge, feeling she had just taken on the whole legal system without any back-up. Maybe she had! So now was the time to get something done. The sooner she sorted it all out, the sooner she could get out of there and start a new life. And it couldn't come quickly enough, as she felt that she was actually beginning to hate a lot of things about Richard and she'd never thought she would ever feel that way about anyone. It wasn't in her nature to hate anyone. She hated the person that he had become; he had changed and she didn't like it at all. He was no longer the charming husband she once knew. He was gone now, and someone else had taken his place!

The atmosphere grew worse every day that passed. Yet Stephanie continued to look after the boys in their usual routine and refused to let Richard get her down. He went to work every day and returned in a foul mood that never seemed to lift at all.

Two days after consulting with a solicitor, Stephanie had a phone call asking her to go into their offices. She had no idea if it was going to go in her favour or not, but she had to find out! That afternoon, the future was in the hands of a total stranger, which was rather hard to accept.

While Stephanie was getting ready for her appointment, Frances answered a knock at the door. It was Laura; she had come by on the chance of catching Stephanie for a quick chat. It was awkward but Stephanie was so pleased to see her best friend; she hadn't had the time to ring her and explain all that had happened lately. In the bedroom where Stephanie was changing, her friend sat and listened to all the awful news about Richard and the affair and how it all tied in with the accident. She also told Laura of how this had changed her and Richard.

Laura burst into tears while Stephanie talked of her plans to leave her beautiful home and go to the States with her mother. Laura couldn't believe what she was hearing; Richard had had a brief affair with another woman? It wasn't Richard's style, and how could he be so careless and cruel?

She would never understand how it had happened to such a wonderful couple. They sat and cried together and hugged each other for a short time, and then Stephanie asked if Laura wanted to go along with her for some support and a little more time together. Laura agreed and they both set out to go and find out what help Stephanie could get with the case.

'I'm sorry you had to go through all this, Steph. I only hope you can get through this thing in one piece, but you know I'm here if you ever need me you know that, don't you?' Laura insisted.

'Of course I do. We've stuck together, you and me, and we will always be the best of friends. Thanks for your support in all this. I really need you here today.' Stephanie was so confident now she had Laura by her side; it was so reassuring for her. This appointment was going to be difficult and it was going to change her whole future forever!

As the two women approached the solicitors' office with a lot of intrepidation, it made Stephanie feel faint at the thought of everything Richard had going for him instead of her. Stephanie had been here several times to discuss the case, and it got harder to understand all this was happening to her and not someone else!

The receptionist was very helpful and directed them both into the waiting room. Stephanie's appointment was next and she began to feel uncomfortable as the hands on the clock ticked by, minute by minute. Suddenly the huge oak door opened and a very tall, thin figure of a man stood in the doorway and said goodbye to his previous client.

'Hello, I'm Andrew Howard. Would you please come into my office?' He was so well mannered and casually dressed for a solicitor.

'Hello. Is it okay if I bring someone with me?'

'I don't see any problem in that, Mrs Sandlers.' He smiled gently as he led the two women out of the waiting room.

Stephanie felt a shiver run down her back as she was referred to as 'Mrs Sandlers'. She no longer wanted Richard's name. She was repulsed by it and intended to change it eventually.

'Please be seated, ladies. We have much to discuss today.'

He was a very attractive man, maybe in his late thirties. Stephanie was sure she saw him pay a lot of attention to Laura, although there wasn't time for flirting.

'Mrs Sandlers, I understand your situation, but there are going to be problems in this case with you against your husband. Now, I can put through your petition for a divorce, but concerning your husband wanting legal custody of your eldest son, he has been granted temporary custody to prevent you leaving the country with both children. I'm so sorry, but he beat you to the mark on this one. I can assure you that it is only temporary.' Mr Howard was very apologetic about the fact that her life had been totally destroyed in a matter of moments in front of her very eyes and she wasn't able to do absolutely anything about it.

Stephanie was absolutely numbed by what Richard had done! He had somehow managed to get custody of Callum before she even knew anything about it and now it was too late to stop him. The whole family had been torn apart, he was to blame, and now he was taking one of their sons away from her too!

Stephanie left the solicitor's shaken and very upset. There was nothing that could be done to reverse the decision; it was out of her hands now. She sobbed her heart out to her friend, who didn't know what to do for the best. Laura walked with her until they got to the car, and then they just sat there holding one another for comfort. Stephanie didn't know what to do next. How could she leave Callum behind? Would Callum want to stay with his father? How could she live without both her sons?

'Oh, my god, Laura what do I do now?' She was desperate for answers.

'Well, if you really want my opinion, I think you should give him hell when you get back. He had no right to do that to you. He could have at least warned you about what you were up against.' Laura was so angry for Stephanie; she felt like hitting Richard when she next saw him. After all, how much lower could he get? Richard was playing dirty now, and it was up to Laura to warn Stephanie to keep her guard up at all times.

Making the decision to leave for the States was more difficult than ever. What would Frances think if Stephanie left one of her sons behind was anyone's guess. Whether the decision was temporary or not, the fact was Richard now had full custody of Callum, so Stephanie's decision either to leave or stay was now insignificant, as Callum was in his father's care and no longer Stephanie's!

The trip back to the house was emotional as Stephanie spent much of her time in tears anyway. She no longer wanted to call it home either; it had been turned into a battleground and war was about to be declared! As the car pulled up in the drive, Stephanie could see Richard was already home from work and it wasn't going to be fun from there onwards.

Stephanie began to shake with anger just at the sight of Richard's car in the drive. Laura and Stephanie locked up the car and went indoors to find Richard in the kitchen talking to her mother. They were so deeply engaged in conversation, that Stephanie stood listening for several minutes without either of them knowing she was there.

'Sorry if I'm interrupting anything, but I would like to have a few private words with Richard.' She was very adamant and distressed.

'I think we'll leave you both alone for a while, Steph.' As Laura and Frances left the kitchen, Frances touched Stephanie's shoulder then gently closed the door behind them. Frances wasn't sure if there was going to be another row, but she knew something was upsetting her daughter yet again.

Both women went and sat in the lounge with Jack and Callum. So much had gone on lately that the two little boys hadn't had the attention they so desperately needed from both parents! It was tough all round for all those involved; anyone who was close to them were playing a part in this fiasco. Callum and Jack were so well behaved it was a pleasure to watch them play together. How was it possible that this perfect family was about to be torn into two directions?

'I'm sorry this is all happening to your family, Frances. Steph deserves better than this and what is about to come out is going to make matters even worse!' Laura felt so upset for her friend.

'What happened today, Laura?' Frances inquired.

'At the solicitor's, Steph was told that Richard had already taken steps to prevent her from taking both boys out of the country. Frances, Richard has full temporary custody of Callum.'

Silence fell upon the two women as they tried to act as normally they could near the boys.

Frances was really astonished at the information she had just heard. 'But he can't do that to my grandchildren. Stephanie couldn't possibly leave one behind. What the hell does he think he's doing, messing with my daughter's life like this?' Now they both knew what Richard was really like. He certainly was showing his true colours now!

Laura heard raised voices coming from the kitchen and knew

one of them was going to explode. Stephanie planned to sort the whole situation by being totally straight with Richard and it was going to get sorted out once and for all. The conflict just had to stop somewhere; it couldn't go on forever. The shouting got louder and louder until there was nothing to be heard. Then there was a loud bang from the kitchen and Stephanie came running into the lounge, looking very distraught!

'Richard has walked out, but not before letting me know where I stand.' She pulled them away from where the boys were sitting and told them that Richard never intended to give Callum up. There was a court order in writing saying that he had temporary custody for three months and then the case would be reviewed. The basis was that the judge thought it unfair of Stephanie to take both to the States and never to return, so this was his judgement!

'What am I going to do, Mom? I can't stay in this nightmare and I can't leave my little boy!'

'My darling, I don't know either, but you are going to have to make a decision sooner or later, and only you can do that.'

'Let's all spend some time with the boys and we'll talk about it later.' Stephanie had so much to concentrate on that she deserved a break, and to relax with her sons. She knew she hadn't spent much time at all with them and wanted to make up for it. They probably had no idea of what was going on anyway, but still she longed to give them what they deserved, a caring mother – although their father would now try to portray her as someone totally different. The paperwork had all been done and there was nothing she could do to reverse the decision. He had really changed, and yet there was no excuse for his behaviour. He wasn't the one who had been left in a coma for weeks. He was the one who had had the affair, not her, yet it was she who was being punished. Why?

As all of them sat down to a civilised dinner together, Stephanie suddenly realised that the following month would be their wedding anniversary. How ironic, she thought.

Chapter Seven

'Mummy, where's Daddy?' Callum quietly asked.

'Daddy had something to do, Callum. I'm sure he'll be back soon. How about we play a game or do something fun after you have finished your meal?' Stephanie was insisting on staying strong for the boys' sake. She made sure they were still in their routine of bath time and meals, and the walks in the park.

Richard didn't come back until the boys had gone to bed that night. He casually walked in and made himself something to eat and stayed in the kitchen out of the way. Stephanie was waiting for him to make some kind of move to make conversation. The boys were in bed and Frances had gone to her room for the evening, too. Now was the right time to get everything out in the open.

Later that evening, they both found themselves in the same room, and forced each other to face the fact that their marriage was over. Not a new fact, but now it seemed so simple just to accept it. The reality of how things had turned out was looking so ugly that neither wanted to admit it.

'So this is what we have come to, is it, Richard?' Stephanie spoke first to clear the air.

'It wouldn't have turned out like this if you hadn't threatened to take my sons to America, Stephanie!' Richard was beginning to raise his voice again, and it unnerved her a little.

'Now listen to me, Richard. I don't know what you think you will achieve by stopping Callum coming with me, but you have to think of what Callum might want to do.'

'I know I've changed there's no need to point that out. I'm not the man you married. Yes, I know the affair and the accident are connected, but I can't change what has happened.' He wasn't at all sympathetic towards her. 'You're making me look like the bad guy here and to be quite honest, I'm getting sick of it all!'

The stress was beginning to show between them both yet

again. Time was getting on and they were both obviously very tired. But one thing had to be said. The time wasn't quite right, but she was going to tell him anyway. 'Richard, I'm still going. I know you have temporary custody of Callum, but I will fight you for him. He should be with me and his little brother. You only did this to me so you're not the loser in this battle. I won't let you humiliate me like this and get away with it. I'm going to make sure I get my son back, whether you like it or not!' She said it and she meant it.

'We'll sit Callum down tomorrow and explain everything to him.' He wanted her to know that he would be there when Callum was told Mummy was leaving!

'I really loved you once, Richard, but now you've destroyed that for me and I'll never be able to forgive you for taking that away from me, along with my son. I despise you for who you have become; you've become selfish and ignorant and your lover is certainly welcome to you, because I don't need you, and I certainly don't feel any love for you any more.'

She felt relieved to have told him how she felt at last and slowly left the room. The next morning at breakfast, everyone sat together and the atmosphere was a lot calmer than usual. Frances pointed out to Stephanie that Laura said to ring her when she had a spare few minutes, even if Laura was at work. Laura wanted to know if she was okay after last night.

Richard felt really uncomfortable, waiting for the right moment to tell Callum of the situation. 'Callum, Mummy and I want to tell you about something very important. We love you very much but we are not going to be able to live together.' He seemed rather upset at looking into his young son's eyes. But not as upset as Stephanie; she looked furious with Richard for speaking first.

'Darling, I have to go away for a while and Daddy is going to look after you for me while I'm away. I want you to know that I love you very much and Daddy will take very good care of you. Do you understand, sweetheart? It won't be for long, and I'll come back and get you and you can come and live with Mummy!' Tears were trickling down her face as she held her son's hand, and looked into his eyes.

'Mummy, I love you too. Can I always stay with Daddy?' His

face, so angelic and innocent, was staring right back at her.

'Of course you can, darling, if that's what you really want.' And with that Stephanie got up from the table and ran out of the kitchen and upstairs to sob her heart out. She hadn't exactly expected his reaction to be quite like that; he knew exactly what he wanted to do. Maybe Richard had somehow managed to fill his tiny head with ideas and things they would do? Who knew? But his mind was made up and so was Richard's.

She spent much of the morning up in her mother's room, sobbing and breaking her heart. She just couldn't believe what was happening to her.

Frances decided to let her son-in-law know exactly what she thought of him. 'I really don't have a lot of things to say to you right now, but I will tell you that you are the most nasty piece of work, and when we leave this house I hope I never set eyes on you again. I hope one day you regret what you have put Stephanie through, and when you do I hope you rot in hell!' After which she left the table and went to see her daughter.

The thought of them staying any longer than they had to didn't look inviting any more to Frances. She could hardly believe how quickly Richard had been able to corrupt Callum into thinking that this was where he was meant to be! Life had been so cruel to her daughter lately that she was sure nothing worse could or would happen to them.

As Frances reached the top of the stairs, she could hear Stephanie breaking her heart. The sobbing was so loud, Frances was afraid the boys might see how upset their mother was, but no one came to her aid. Frances was unsure whether to disturb Stephanie or just to let her get it out of her system. After all, there wasn't much more Frances could do, as she had let Richard know just how she felt about the whole situation.

The only thing left to do was to get away from all the bad feeling that surrounded them. It was a suffocating feeling that they had to escape from. While Frances stood pondering the future, there was a weak voice trying to reach out for help.

'Mom, is that you?' Stephanie whispered through the door.

'Yes, it is. Can I come in, darling?' Frances asked gently. 'I'm so sorry Callum said those dreadful things to you, my dear, but at least you know now where you stand, and you can get on with organising your own life. I'm sure that Richard will find it no easy task, looking after a young child on his own, and when he comes to his senses he will be begging you to come and collect Callum and everything will be as they should.' Frances tried her hardest to persuade Stephanie that was how it was all going to work out.

Although there was method in how Richard was going about this, he was aware he would be able to get out of paying so much money to Stephanie if he had one of his children, and he would also be due some of her future income to support him and Callum. Nothing was stopping him from giving up work altogether and looking after Callum as a full-time father.

But now it all seemed to sink in to Stephanie that she had to let go now, and let things take their natural course. Who knew what might happen when they turned a corner. They sat next to each other and comforted each other as they had done quite a lot recently. It was all they had now. Without her mother, Stephanie would have found herself in a most difficult situation.

The next few days were very hard for Stephanie as she and her young son were preparing to fly out to the States and there wasn't a lot of time for her to spend with Callum. The strain was beginning to show and she didn't feel she could take any more. Stephanie had been in touch with her friend Laura and told her of the situation and what had been decided, and how Richard had managed to get their son to stay with his father.

Laura was disgusted at the manner in which he had been conducting himself of late! But it was nothing to do with her, she knew that, and all she could do was support her best friend in whatever she decided. No matter how difficult things might get, Laura assured Stephanie she would always be there for her.

It was now only two days to their departure and Stephanie opted for a few peaceful hours with her sons alone, so they could talk and laugh and sing little songs and, most importantly, to let the two young boys spend some real time together before Richard could spoil that too. She decided to take them to a really beautiful park she knew. There was an adventure playground for Callum to play in and they could just relax. It was a beautiful September afternoon, and the sun was glowing in the warm September breeze. It had rained in the night and the ground was still damp, and Callum had made sure he didn't leave the house without his green wellingtons, and ran through the leaves on the ground and gave little fits of giggles. Jack sat in his stroller and watched his big brother with envy and waved his tiny hands in the air.

They both loved the great outdoors, and she made sure they got some fresh air every day. The crisp sound of leaves being crushed beneath Callum's feet was magical and it was so much fun. She found herself thinking of all the good times they had had together as a family, and how things were going to change dramatically from how they usually were.

But that was then and she was here and had to concentrate on now and where she would begin to try to make Callum realise she would always love him, and he was to be a good boy for his father. Where was she to begin? As Callum started to run towards her, Stephanie knelt down and threw her arms open to catch the incoming bundle of joy. She gathered him up in her arms and held him tight for what seemed like ages, and as she put him down she whispered, 'I love you.' As she did so, he looked into his mother's eyes and hugged her tightly, so she knew he loved her too!

Stephanie took the stroller and walked through the park and she put a little warm blanket in the stroller to keep Jack warm, as there was a slight breeze in the air. As they approached a seating area, Stephanie encouraged Callum to sit down and have a drink and a packet of crisps. Timing was everything and she wanted to do this right for both their sakes, as she needed to know Callum fully understood what was going to happen. She wasn't going to let Richard make her be the baddie and for him to come up smelling of roses. She had learned to handle herself assertively and keep her confidence.

'Callum, do you know why Mummy will be going away?' Stephanie had said it and wasn't quite sure how he would respond.

'You're going to live with Grandma, but I want to live here with Daddy. I love you, Mummy, and Jack. You come home soon?'

Tears were streaming down her face as she looked at her son

and nodded her head. She didn't know how long it would be before she got the chance to come back to visit, but she would do everything she could to keep in touch with him. After the most awkward questions were out the way, they relaxed and talked more, Callum told his little brother to be good and go to sleep at night. Callum was a sensible boy and talked a lot about his little brother. Everyone at nursery knew all about Jack and what he got up to at home. Stephanie found that a real comfort as she was sure Callum wouldn't forget Jack!

As the leaves began to fall, Stephanie realised this was probably the last time she would get to see Callum jumping through the leaves enjoying himself, for a long time. It was hard to accept, but Stephanie had this time with him and he was having so much fun and giggling to himself as he ran through the park. That afternoon her life became so much clearer and she now felt at ease with herself. It was fun and calming, just her and her two sons. Tomorrow was to be a morning with herself and Frances with the boys before they left for the airport!

That evening, the mood in the family home was somewhat solemn and distant. But it was to be expected, as the ever-impending separation between mother and son became imminent. Stephanie had to somehow find the strength to get through the night and to make her departure as least painful as possible, yet she doubted in her own mind if she was really doing the right thing, by her or by Callum.

Did Callum have any idea just how long his mother would be away from him and how long it would be before he got to see her again? Stephanie was so confused that night when she went to bed; there had been so much happening in such little time, she couldn't take it all in. The fact that she was getting out of a rotten marriage was the only reason she could think of, right now, for her to be behaving in such a manner. But when she did return to gain back her son, would he still love her like he'd said, or would his attitude have changed towards her?

There were no answers to this endless puzzle, only new riddles she couldn't possibly resolve! As she kissed her two sons in their beds, she realised just how much they would both change over the next few months, and she wondered to herself how they would feel at being separated. Could they ever be normal brothers, after she left one of them behind?

As Stephanie turned to leave their rooms, she sensed Richard was nearby, and as she looked up their eyes met for a brief moment, but there was no feeling between them. That had long gone – the love, the trust, and the romance, everything that a marriage meant to her anyway! Stephanie felt as if Richard had come to check up on her. She wanted to tell him that he was invading her space, that he didn't have any right over her children whatsoever. But she knew he would probably just laugh at her, so she just starred right through him as though he wasn't there at all.

'What's the rush, Steph, got a plane to catch?' His words were like venom, yet he looked very pleased with the remark he had just made.

'You disgust me, do you know that, Richard? How dare you?' And, just as he turned away, Stephanie raised her left hand and swiftly dragged it across her husband's face.

He was taken by total and utter surprise, as he didn't think she was capable of violence.

Stephanie had never hit Richard before during their brief marriage. But this was how far he had pushed her. She wasn't going to stand for it any longer, even if she had to result to violence! 'You're right about one thing, Richard, I *do* have a plane to catch – but don't think for a minute you will ever get permanent custody of Callum, never in a million years.' As Stephanie said all this, she made sure her son's doors were closed tightly, so as not to disturb them and they couldn't hear any of the commotion going on!

'You seem so sure of yourself, Steph, but just remember you are leaving me, not the other way around. I know all the rules, and if I can I will break them.'

Stephanie pushed by him to get to the stairs. She felt the sudden urge to hit him again, but managed to contain her anger in time. She went downstairs instead to get away from him. She just couldn't bear to be near him or look at him. As she reached the bottom of the stairs, she looked towards the kitchen for her mother and found Frances listening to every word that had been said between them.

'I am so sorry, Stephanie. He's really done the best he can to make you feel unwanted in your own home. I think you are doing the right thing tomorrow by coming home with me.'

The two women stood and wept in each other's arms, and sighed at the thought of leaving, but it was the best thing to do. After all Richard was making life for her near impossible to stay.

Richard never came downstairs that night; he went to his room and didn't come out again. Frances stayed up until nearly everything had been packed and organised. It was the least she could do for her daughter and grandson. Stephanie continued to pack clothes and toys, and as she did she began to sob quietly enough to not interrupt Frances. There had been too many tears in that house and it was beginning to grind Stephanie down. She was absolutely exhausted, to say the least, but she kept going for the sake of her children.

By the time they had both finished organising everything for the following day, it was early morning, and they decided to get what sleep they could. Nobody slept that night, and even though Stephanie was leaving, the boys were understandably calm and happy. To her they were making the most of what little time they had together. They all looked extremely tired and stressed, but that was down to all the pressure they had been under for the past few weeks.

Stephanie tried to keep herself busy most of the morning, as she didn't want to upset her sons more than need be. Richard managed to avoid all confrontation with his wife and went around the house as his usual moody self! That was the way they had come to know him now, moody and so different to how he used to be around his family. Stephanie did her best to organise the rest of her time around everyone else, and there was one last thing to do; she had to ring Laura and say her goodbyes. She phoned Laura but there was no answer, so she left a message on her machine, letting her know what time her flight was leaving and she was deeply sorry she hadn't seen her before going!

It broke her heart, but she had to hide her unhappiness so Richard didn't see. Jack was ready and packed to go, and as the time drew nearer to leave Callum hugged his mother and told her he loved her and he wanted her to come home soon. Little did he know what was really going on; if he did he would have wanted to go with her! But his father put a stop to that almost instantly, so Callum didn't find out the truth.

Frances had nothing at all to say to her son-in-law, but gave him a look that made him feel incredibly uncomfortable.

'Mom, I'm just going to take a look around to check I have everything before I leave,' Stephanie said sadly.

'Okay, Stephanie, but the cab will be here in thirty minutes.'

They both knew it would probably be the last time she saw her home for quite some time. It was time to say goodbye to the beautiful home she adored so much and brought her children up in. Tears streamed down her face as she wandered into every room to look around and remember.

The pain of all that had happened cut through her like an invisible knife, and she felt so hurt by it all. But she was moving on now. Time to start a new life, a new home and make the most of what she had. As she came down the stairs one last time, she wiped away the tears and once again hid the heartache. Everybody gathered in the hall to say their goodbyes, and each in turn gave Callum and his brother big hugs and plenty of kisses. It was truly the hardest moment in Stephanie's life. She couldn't bear the pain of it, and she burst into tears again.

Richard stood in the background, witnessing the grief he'd caused, and the hurt and the pain. His face was slightly gaunt, looking as if he regretted his actions. But he didn't even offer to help with their luggage. He was too much of a coward to even do that. As he stood and watched his wife break away from her eldest son, he turned away so as not to see her. It was too late now for any changes. After the hatred she had seen inside him, she no longer loved him, and they both knew that.

The cab pulled up onto the drive in front of the house on the close and the driver politely knocked on the front door. 'Cab for the airport, Madam?' he said, feeling awkward at the sight that greeted him at the door.

'Yes, that's right. Could you take the luggage, please?' Frances asked the driver, who was more than helpful, but didn't say more than that.

Jack began to sense the atmosphere and began to cry. He

didn't understand what was going on as he was the only four months old. How could any of them explain it to him?

'Well, Callum, I have to go now. I love you so dearly, my darling little son. Now you be a good little boy while Mummy is away. And I want you to know I will call you as soon as I get to Grandma's. Anyway, you have to look after your father while I'm gone. He's got to behave, too, you know!'

Callum giggled at what his mother had said and jumped up to give her a final hug and kiss. 'I love you too, Mummy. I'll see you soon, and I love Jack, too.'

As she put her son down, she glanced around to look for Richard in the kitchen. She just wanted to hear maybe 'sorry' or at least goodbye, but he couldn't even bring himself to look at her. So she kissed Callum one last time and carried Jack in her arms and turned her back on her old home and life to get into the cab.

Frances had already done everything else, now it was her turn. It broke her heart to know Callum wasn't going with them, as she wasn't sure when she would get to see him again. She hugged the life out of the little soul and planted great big kisses all over his angelic little face. 'Always remember we all love you very much, sweetheart. Come and see us soon, all right?'

And as she turned to leave she broke down in tears and ran to the cab!

The journey to the airport was very strange and hardly a word was spoken. Both women didn't stop sobbing until they were literally at the airport. Little Jack sat so silently in his mother's arms, just staring into her eyes. It was almost like he understood his mothers' pain. As Stephanie wiped the tears from her eyes, she gazed into her son's face and stroked his hair and smiled gently at him. She felt thankful she had him with her and hadn't lost both boys to her husband. The whole world she had ever known had crumbled and disappeared, and now it was her job to take control of her life and start a new life with her baby son.

Alone with only her mother to lean on, Stephanie felt somehow bewildered at what lay ahead in the life she had chosen. Frances gently glanced their way, and touched Stephanie's hand as tears welled in her eyes once again. The reunion of mother and daughter hadn't expected to end by returning home with a broken-hearted daughter from a lost marriage.

As the cab driver pulled into the airport, Frances thanked him and asked only for his assistance in taking the luggage through the heaving crowd of travellers. Stephanie and her mother and little Jack were left standing on their own, and Stephanie was looking like a nervous wreck by then. The airport was choking with holidaymakers and businessmen. The noise was unbearable with speakers shouting announcements for arrivals and departures.

They both checked in for their flight and together they went for a coffee in the restaurant. Jack had been so good for his mother that they hardly knew he was there. He had his afternoon bottle and change and fell asleep while his mother and grandma enjoyed a coffee together. The conversation was limited as both were too upset to talk of the day's events. But as time drew nearer they took a walk towards the departure lounge, ready for their flight. There was an intense feeling of sadness and loneliness as Stephanie watched a couple saying their goodbyes to what looked like their son as he embarked on a trip without them! Her feelings had so much in common with his, as he was leaving what looked like loved ones behind.

Stephanie's heart began to race faster as a young family entered the lounge with three young children. She couldn't help noticing the couple looked so loving and so together. Maybe it was jealousy of how they were and how she and Richard should have been. But as she turned her head she felt a lump in her throat; it was all too emotional for her. Her face was so pale and ill-looking; she hadn't really put any effort into dressing for her new life. It seemed pointless trying to impress herself or anyone else when she felt so unattractive and, even though she was no longer tied to a relationship, she didn't want any interest going in her favour.

As Stephanie, Jack and Frances sat listening and watching, there was a distant sound of someone shouting a name. Neither of them could identify what it was, but it was someone's name. It took their interest instantly. And through the crowd Stephanie was sure she saw a friendly face; it was her only best friend in the world, Laura Colt. Laura had missed them leaving home, so she'd decided to follow them to the airport to say goodbye.

It was such a relief to find her in time before she left for the

States. 'God, I thought I'd never see you again, Steph!' Laura grabbed her best friend and hugged her so tightly, as if she was afraid to let go.

'Oh, Laura, am I glad to see you, you don't know how awful it's been at the house. Richard was so nasty, and I had to leave my little Callum behind because of him.' Stephanie was absolutely distraught and fretful.

Frances stood back with Jack and watched her daughter and her friend talk of the previous few days. It was so hard for Stephanie to get all her grief and pain out and tell her friend the terrible truth that her marriage was over.

Laura found all the news very disturbing and cried for Stephanie. She hated to see someone she cared so much for in so much pain. How dared Richard treat her like that? Who did he think he was? She was feeling angry towards Richard; he had forced Stephanie out of her home and also out of the country, as she felt she couldn't bear to be near him.

After a while they all sat down together to talk about their future plans for America, but it didn't look as if they would be coming back for quite some time, even years!

'Will you promise me you'll keep an eye on Callum for me, please? I don't know when I'll get to see him again. Richard made it impossible for me to bring him with me. Richard was so nasty about it all. I don't know him any more Laura.' Stephanie tried to explain the whole situation since the last time she was at the house.

'Stephanie, you can count on me. I will let you know how things are going, this end. He will not get away with the way he treated you, my dear friend.' Laura used her words wisely and let Stephanie know exactly how she felt about Richard.

An announcement broadcasting the final departure for New York came swiftly on time. The two friends couldn't bear to let go, but knew they would have to go their separate ways. Goodbyes were not a strong point with Laura; she made a point of reminding Stephanie to ring when they arrived in New York, to let her know they had landed safely. The whole scene was very heartbreaking.

As Frances carried Jack toward the terminal, the emotion took over and the two friends were torn apart. Flight attendants stood waiting for passengers to board at the gates and, as Stephanie left the warm embrace of her life-long friend, her face flushed with the tears of sadness. Time was running out as they parted ways, and a last gesture by Laura, the symbol of a phone call, could be recognised by Stephanie and she responded by nodding her head.

As the final passenger passed through the gates, Laura sat down and wept. She just couldn't understand why it had all happened.

Settling Jack was a little stressful on boarding the plane. He had simply never flown before and he was a little uneasy about all the fuss. He was made to feel as comfortable as they could possibly be made. It was going to be an interesting flight, especially with such a young baby!

Stephanie felt numb all over, and she hadn't wanted to make any conversation at all. She was lost in her own thoughts for what seemed like most of the flight. Frances felt very much alone and silent, lost for words; how her daughter must be feeling was unbearable. There was no way she could ever be able to understand the sequence of events that led to this.

Jack slept soundly for most of the time, while his mother was lost in a world of thought. She would have to explain all of this one day, but for now she would let him sleep; after all sleeping was one of Jacks many talents and she never woke him from a peaceful slumber! It was so hard not to think of who she had left behind, how it was all going to be so different from the moment she'd walked out of the door. Stephanie's new life lay ahead and as she gazed out the window, she wondered how her sons' lives were going to be changed forever.

Thoughts were swimming around her head like an ocean of dreams, ideas of a new beginning she had never dreamed of. This could be the very thing she had needed and it was thanks to Richard that she had discovered it!

'Stephanie, dear, how are you feeling? I don't want to upset you but I'm so worried for you, you have hardly said a word through the entire flight!'

Frances looked at her daughter and held her hand for comfort.

'Oh, Mom, I just wish I knew what was going to happen next. It's all so confusing right now. But we will be all right won't we,

Jack?' As Stephanie looked down at her little son, he gazed back and gave her a little smile.

The flight had seemed endless, but as they sat next to each other they knew they were going to be there for each other no matter what.

Frances had already worked out that they were going to be picked up at the airport by a close friend, and taken back to her home in New York. In the light of recent events, Frances was definitely looking forward to being back home again. She dearly loved to visit Stephanie and her family, but the past couple of weeks had been a strain on all those involved, including Frances herself. What remained now was for her to get Stephanie and Jack settled in her home and try to make life as normal as possible for them both. She knew it wasn't going to be easy but Frances enjoyed fresh challenges.

As the plane began to prepare its passengers for landing, Frances helped Stephanie settle Jack down in his own baby seat and tried to play with him so he wouldn't really notice they were landing!

The flight had been very relaxing and an enjoyable experience. Jack had been delightful during the flight and had been no real trouble at all. It was a good start for a new beginning. The plane landed on American soil and it was a truly exciting experience for Stephanie and Jack. This was one place that Stephanie would soon learn to love and live among a more casual society, and she was already enjoying the atmosphere among the other passengers who were also visiting the States!

It was a huge airport and so busy it was frightening. The usual noise and atmosphere was so much more boring compared to the American airport, it was full of international visitors and lots of children running around their parents.

When they reached the arrivals lounge they sat down and just waited for Frances's friend to come and collect them. Corrine had been a good friend to Frances since they first met several years ago, when they'd moved into the same neighbourhood. She had also been good company for Frances when Harry had passed away. They were very close and had never let each other down. That was what friends were for and Frances thought a great deal of Corrine.

Travelling had worn Stephanie out and little Jack, who could barely open his eyes, he was so tired. After coming through customs it was good to sit down for a few minutes. Although the arrivals lounge was a little quieter, Stephanie couldn't relax properly until she knew they were at her mother's home on 53rd and West Avenue, New York. Frances was on the look-out for Corrine who'd said she would be there when they all arrived – and, true to her word, she walked into the area where she was told they would be waiting!

'Hello, Frances, I hope you had a safe journey home?' Corrine was a very casual-looking lady who seemed very confident and very lively looking for her age. She was just slightly younger than Frances.

'Hi, Corrine, let me introduce you to my daughter Stephanie and my grandson Jack.'

The conversation was polite yet short as Corrine knew there were complications and didn't wish to put her foot in her mouth. Corrine seemed a very nice friend of her mothers and it was also clear to Stephanie that Corrine worried about Frances. She looked tired and exhausted as they all left the airport, and it was Corrine who said so. Going home was going to be wonderful, as Frances hadn't told Stephanie just how much she had missed being there.

'So this is your newest grandson, Frances. Isn't he a handsome little boy?' Corrine didn't want to intrude any further as she didn't want to upset anyone's feelings.

'Well, he looks just like his older brother. I'm sure you will get to meet him soon, once we are all settled.'

Stephanie was a little choked but managed to keep it under control. It certainly wasn't going to be smooth running at the beginning, but when people got to know her and Jack she was quite sure it would all work out pretty well.

They were only half an hour away from home when Stephanie realised just how long it had been since she had been to the big city. It was totally amazing, the sights she saw. Although it was a little daunting at first, Stephanie seemed sure she would be able to make a life for herself here. Everywhere she looked there were people; the streets were almost overcrowded with people shopping and going to work and children running to catch the bus to school. This new lifestyle was definitely going to be busier than living in little old England.

As the car came to a stand still, Stephanie remembered her mother's home and as she gazed out of the window she knew that this was where she truly belonged!

Chapter Eight

This was to be her and Jack's home now. Throughout this whole terrible ordeal she had come to trust her instincts and make the right decisions over her life. She was in control for the first time in so long that she liked it, it felt so good. She could be her own person at last. The initial impact of no longer being a married woman and moving from one country to another was hard to take in but Stephanie now knew that she was solely in charge of what would happen now and there would be no more deceiving or lying from this point on. She was free to do what she wanted to be without any interference from Richard or anyone else, for that matter.

Walking into her mother's home, she could still smell her childhood in the house as though it already had Stephanie living there! It felt slightly odd as it had been some time since she had been there.

Corrine made herself useful immediately and made them all a drink. She had kept a close watch over the house, as Frances had asked, and she had brought fresh groceries from the Deli near by, so they didn't have to go out when they came home.

'Well, Jack, darling, this is where Grandma lives and we are going to live here with her, what do you think?'

Gurgling was all he could manage, but that was good enough for his mother; she knew he liked being there too. Life on 53rd and West Avenue was going to be a lot more fun and a new chance to make a new life for her and her sons.

Callum was constantly on her mind and she needed to unwind from the journey before embarking on the mission of calling Richard so she could speak to Callum. After all, he hadn't even been able to bring himself to apologise or even offer help to put her luggage in the cab! He no longer figured in her life any more, the damage had been done and it was never going to be repaired.

She stopped thinking of it all and took Jack outside into the beautiful garden that her mother loved so much. Sadly Harry was no longer there to see just how well she had nurtured it. Harry had always loved this garden and it was easy to see why; it had just blossomed with every flower he had planted and in a way it was still Harry's garden.

By now it was getting late into the evening and the jet lag was beginning to show on all of them. Corrine had long gone; she only lived three houses away so she was really close by. She also happened to be a widow herself, so she and Frances had much in common, only Corrine never had any children, but she never made a big deal out of it. She had had a good life and a wonderful husband, and she had been very satisfied with that!

Frances thought highly of her and had often spoke about Corrine over the phone; they shared trips and went out to the theatre a lot. It was companionship for the two women. On the whole, Frances had managed to keep it together when Harry, Stephanie's father, passed on, as though she knew that Corrine would be there for her should she need anything.

Whereas Stephanie had lost it totally when her world had fallen apart. It was strange how a mother and daughter coped with these situations so differently! It wasn't important now; what mattered now was getting her life as normal as possible.

After putting Jack down in the crib that she had been put to lie in as a baby, Stephanie was able to think about making the awkward phone call to England to speak to her other son before Richard had time to brainwash him into thinking that she was gone forever or something like that. She knew too well just what he was capable of doing. The excitement had long since calmed in the house and now it was time to make the call. As she waited to be connected she wandered what the reaction would be. She didn't know if he would let her speak to Callum alone or if he would be listening in on the conversation!

A voice reached out on the connecting line; it was not as sharp as she had expected him to be towards her.

'Richard, you sound different. We have arrived safely. I thought I'd ring to let Callum know we are well and we love him and miss him dreadfully.'

Silence struck the conversation and it almost became too

unbearable, but she insisted that he speak to her, no matter how she felt about him now!

It was what she had been dreading, this kind of attitude over the phone; he was still making her feel uncomfortable.

'Were you aware that he hasn't slept at all through the night? He's been waiting to hear your voice.'

It was unbelievable. Richard was actually making her look like the monster in all this, and he truly made his son believe that his mother couldn't care less about him! It was utterly cruel and mean to do such a thing to a young child like Callum. 'Are you going to let me talk to my son or not?' she snapped.

'Mummy, Mummy, you said you were going to ring me. I love you, Mummy. Where's Jack?' His little voice echoed down the telephone line; it ripped her heart out just to hear him so distressed and tearful. Just what had his father been telling him when she'd finally left?

'Oh, Callum, Mummy and Jack love you so much. We really do miss you terribly. I hope you have been a good boy for Daddy. Has Laura been to see you, darling?' she said.

'Laura came and played with me and gave me dinner.' Tears streamed down his face as he thought of his mummy; it had upset him, all this change and he was a little lost as this had never happened before. Mummy had never left him behind before, only to have Jack in hospital.

'Stephanie, Callum is really upset now. Can you call him again when he isn't so tired? I only let you speak to him because he has been waiting for your call.'

It was the tone she had come to despise in Richard, cold and ignorant!

She was in tears as he told her when she could and couldn't speak to her own son. 'Please, at least let me say goodbye to Callum, Richard!'

As he gave the phone to Callum, she could hear whispering going on in the background.

'I have to go now, Callum, darling, but Mummy loves you lots and so does Jack. We will ring you again soon. You can send me some pictures and things you do at playgroup if you want to as well. You could get Laura to help you if you want to, sweetheart, she would love that. Bye, now. Be good for me.' It broke her heart to leave him with only a few words to say, but at least Richard had let her speak to her son for a while.

Frances saw the state she was in after the phone call and tried to console her broken daughter. There was little she could do but comfort her and offer support in any way she could! After telling her mother what Callum had said, Stephanie smiled and reminded her mother that she knew he was being well looked after and she would get him back one day.

The two exhausted women went to bed, feeling utterly shattered and drained from the day's events. But tomorrow would be a new day full of new experiences for Stephanie and Jack and just maybe they could at last begin their new life!

As autumn turned to winter, the Christmas season was beginning to close in around Stephanie. This was to be the first Christmas without Callum or her husband. The thought of it sent shivers down her spine; being thousands of miles away from her eldest child seemed unbearable and distressing. She was on her own now and it was up to her to make the best of the situation. The fact that it was also Jack's first ever Christmas and it was in a place where he didn't recognise or had any choice in being there – it had to be Fate. However could Stephanie explain it, otherwise?

The atmosphere over there at Christmas time was magical and fantastic; Stephanie began to take Jack to all the activities she could, including Father Christmas in the biggest department store she had ever been in! Jack's whole face lit up with wonder at the bearded old man dressed in red and white; he was amazed. The lights and window themes created a winter wonderland for all to enjoy for the festive season. Frances had organised a special meal for a few friends to come over and celebrate Christmas and especially to welcome Stephanie and Jack. After all, they were there to give a helping hand if she was ever to need one. Frances's friends were all very special and were always there for her in times of trouble and she relied on them all greatly at times!

That evening went very smoothly and without any problems and Jack delighted all the guests that evening. He had turned seven months just a few days before and was changing all the time. He was going to be such a handsome young boy just like his elder brother!

Richard had been very slack in sending photos of Callum and it deeply hurt Stephanie as she longed to be with her darling little boy again. She wasn't able to make plans yet to go and visit, as she and Jack had barely time to settle over there! It was so awkward and frustrating for Jack and Frances, too. Richard was playing games with their emotions and they weren't too sure how much longer he was going to continue to be so cruel.

Stephanie had heard from Laura, who always said things were good and there was no bad feeling between her and Richard. Stephanie missed Laura dreadfully, too, but at least they could call or write!

Christmas crept away as slowly as it had come and it was a new year with all its glory and new beginnings. It wasn't going to be special at all for Stephanie as she had nothing to plan, apart from trying to get over to see Callum as soon as she could. The last few months had been terrible, although she tried to hide it from her mother; she couldn't bear to see her hurt more than she had been recently.

Frances had noticed a little sadness but knew there was just cause, as she also knew that it was impossible to leave a country with only one of two children and not be expected to pick up the pieces of a failed marriage without so much as a broken heart.

The phone calls continued to Callum after a few strong words with Richard in the new year. It was a strange sensation on the phone one evening, as Richard kept talking to her for what seemed like an hour and Stephanie thought it was very odd. What was Richard up to? He normally only had time to say a few words before Callum had the phone. Stephanie asked to speak to Callum and was left feeling as though something was wrong because of the way Richard was actually being very pleasant to her.

Callum was delightful to speak to and he managed to tell his mummy all about his Christmas gifts and where he had been and what his daddy had been doing over the holidays, she knew he had had a really good Christmas. But she missed him terribly and concealed her hurt until she put the phone down and collapsed into a flood of tears!

The sun rose to shine through a very bright breakfast room. It was one of the rooms in her mother's home that Stephanie liked the most. All three of them sat around the table eating pancakes and toast; it was relaxing and homely. 'Mom, today I'm going to put my life and Jack's into perspective and start anew.' It was a rather shocking start to the morning conversation, but that was how Stephanie was feeling.

'Well, I must say, you certainly took long enough to make that statement, dear.'

'I feel as if much of my life has been wasted running after Richard and being there for him. I think it's time I did something for me, and that means getting a new life without Richard Sandlers.' Stephanie was beginning to feel she had complete control over her life for the first time in years. She had always thought she was happy with everything that she could ever want but it had all been just an illusion!

She had been kidding herself. She had been there for Richard, but where had he been? Having an affair! How many more had there been that she didn't know about? She had lived her married life not knowing just what he was doing to her. It had been all so very low-key and secretive that she would never known about the affair at all if his other woman hadn't caused the accident.

Over the rest of breakfast Stephanie laid out her plans to her mother and explained that she had to do something more with her life. Stephanie now wanted her career back; she wanted new friends and a new life for her and Jack and eventually Callum. She had very carefully thought it all through, and she didn't intend on living off Frances, either. Stephanie insisted that she was going to go to work to maintain a lifestyle for her and Jack!

Weeks went by and Stephanie began searching for the job she had been trained for, a fashion expert. She had got a degree in design back in university and had had a reasonably paid job, which suited her in every respect, but had given it all up to pursue a family lifestyle. A new life was being mapped out in America.

Richard was trying to cope alone with his eldest son. It was certainly a new challenge, and one he deeply began to regret. How stupid he had been to be so selfish and rude to Stephanie. But it had been the male pride in him that had prevented him from telling his wife just how he felt. Instead Richard had driven her from her home and out of the country! Richard was alone now, with the fear of not being able to come to terms with the fact that he alone had ruined his life, his marriage and his wife! A stupid affair that had spelled disaster from the very beginning. If only he had resisted the temptation of another woman at the time when his wife needed him most, when she was pregnant with their second son!

It had been a very selfish thing to do and he wasn't sure how he was going to repair the damage but maybe one day he would certainly try.

Their Christmas had been as pleasant as Richard could have made it, and it was with a little help from Laura that when eventually Christmas came they tried to make it every bit the fun time that they usually enjoyed together, but it was also obvious that something special was missing and they all knew what it was!

Richard had sent lots of gifts over to Stephanie for her and Jack, labelled them from Callum, but it was not the most normal of situations at all. The first Christmas had been enough without either of them, but how many could both of them take before the whole thing got too ridiculous?

The New Year came and went and this time there was no one to keep Richard company, except Callum. It spelled the start of a new life of a father and son together. Callum would be almost four and it would be playgroup almost every day then for him, and that would make things much easier for Richard! He had his job to consider and the company were not going to be as lenient with him for much longer in the circumstances surrounding his marriage!

Chapter Nine

Both sides of the divided family were getting on with their lives and the divorce papers arrived, which made it all seem so final. But there was the matter of the accident and whether anything would come out in favour of a prosecution; it was a slow process but it had to finish soon!

Stephanie would never forget the fact that it was all Michaela's fault and because of that this was the result! She was only too glad she hadn't been killed, or even worse, the children. It was miraculous just how her husband had totally escaped injury, yet she had fallen into a coma for two weeks. There were endless questions still going round her head, and she knew the nightmare of the actual accident would probably never go away.

After a particularly hard day at the office, Richard had arrived home to find the divorce papers on the doormat. Not the warm greeting he would have liked but that was the way it was. Callum had been at the local crèche where he really enjoyed the company of other children. Richard fixed them a quick meal and sat with his son for a while. They got on quite well, considering that his mother had left, but it suited them both to live like this – for a while, anyway!

'Do you want me to read to you tonight, Callum, or do you just want to go in the bath and then bed?' Richard had begun to take on both parental roles and tried to help Callum as much as possible.

'Read to me tonight, Daddy, a good story.'

Callum was a brilliantly behaved young boy and, although they had grown to learn to live on their own, the bond between them was still there; it had never gone away!

Richard put Callum to bed for the evening and sat in the lounge with a coffee, pondering over the large brown envelope that he had previously placed on the coffee table. Although he knew just exactly what it was, he still hesitated to open it. This was his entire fault and now it had ended in one document! As he leaned over to pick it up, he had a feeling of guilt and an overwhelming feeling of panic and remorse over his recent behaviour. He had truly changed over these past few months. Could it be really possible that everything was about to change for the better?

Stephanie had stated in the divorce papers that she was going to pursue the custody battle over Callum, even though she knew the boy wanted to stay with his father. As Richard read further into the documentation, he realised that this wasn't what he wanted at all. He wanted to be happy again and live with a complete family, not just half! He put the papers down and decided to call his soon to be ex-wife, Stephanie. It was as though he had only just put his life into perspective; he wanted Stephanie back and he wanted her to know that.

The call was going to come as a surprise to Stephanie, as Richard had not actually shared his feelings with her for so long. 'Hello, is that you, Stephanie? It's me, Richard.' If you rang this number, then you had better go through with what you really want to say, thought Richard to himself. But this time it was his heart that was ruling his head, so he knew he had to tell her how he felt.

'Richard, do you have any idea what time it is? What do you want?' Stephanie was in no mood for an argumentative conversation with Richard, as she knew only too well that he had probably received his papers by now! Although it was a long-distance call, Richard didn't have a care in the world what time it was over there and he began to babble on about how stupid he had been and he wished everything was the way it used to be.

Explaining to Stephanie just how different he was, and that he regretted everything that had happened between them, was hard to do, and as silence fell on the other end of the line Richard was sure that Stephanie was listening carefully to what he had to say. It was early evening where Richard was, but it was a totally different time zone where Stephanie was, but that didn't bother Richard!

'Richard, what is it you really want? I am tired and you will wake my mom if you continue to call at this ungodly hour!'

Stephanie was getting fed up listening to the meaningless words of her husband!

'Stephanie, I want you to know how I feel about you. I never meant to hurt you at all. I miss you so much and so does Callum. We want you to come home, Steph. I don't care about the divorce papers: who can blame you for that?'

Richard was getting distressed at that point of the conversation. He wanted his wife back and he was almost begging her over the phone, but little did he realise that Stephanie had begun a whole new life and what mattered to her now was moving on and starting a new life with her baby son Jack, and eventually gaining her other son Callum back in her custody!

'Richard, I think you should call me another time. You aren't thinking straight. You just received your divorce papers and you are grasping at straws now, and it isn't fair on me or you to continue with this conversation. Anyway, I would like to talk to Callum when you call again!' After trying to reason with Richard, Stephanie put the phone down and stood in the hall for a while, trying to understand the whole call.

Richard also put the phone down and literally kicked himself for almost breaking down on the phone. He hadn't wanted to sound as desperate as he had. He slowly made his way up the stairs to look in on Callum, to assure himself he hadn't woken the boy with the phone call. As he opened the door to Callum's room, he glanced over to the bed and saw his son sleeping soundly, tucked in the way his father had left him that evening. Callum was a picture of innocence, even when he was asleep.

After a while, Richard left the sleeping toddler and went back downstairs to consider his next move to gain back his wife.

He'd never thought for one moment just how things were going to be so different for them both. Richard wasn't sure if it was the new year blues he was feeling or if it was the idea of going through a whole new year without the people he loved the most. Work was certainly taking his mind off the situation but it wasn't solving the problem. Colleagues of Richard didn't know the full extent of the damage he had caused his family, but it wasn't any of their business anyway.

Richard sat in the lounge for the remainder of the evening and tried to think of a solution to the trouble he had caused. Maybe he should consider moving to the States to try to win his wife back, and they could all start a fresh life with a new beginning – but would Stephanie want that? Richard's mind was buzzing with ideas and he wanted to do something about it while he could, especially now he had declared his feelings for Stephanie and she now knew just what was going on. It was nearly 3 a.m. before Richard went to his bed as he had spent the whole evening working out the idea of moving to the States to be near Stephanie and Jack. This was one idea that he was beginning to like the sound of, the more he thought of it. And there was really no way that Stephanie could stop him!

It was a few days later after the conversation with Stephanie that Richard received a phone call from his solicitor, saying that Michaela Stornton had been found guilty in court of reckless driving. She had been given a hefty fine and the court had also revoked her licence for a period of fourteen months. So there it was, all concluded in the loss of a driving licence: it was over and it couldn't have come at a better time than this. Richard was at last able to pick up the discarded pieces of his life and begin again. Michaela Stornton had never figured in his life or was ever going to mean anything to Richard. A stupid fling was all it had been, nothing more!

Richard called Stephanie that instant to express how glad he was, at it all being finished with, and that he never wanted to hear Michaela's name mentioned ever again! The conversation lifted his spirits and for a rather weak moment Richard felt so tempted to tell her of his impending plan to move nearer her and Jack, but he stopped himself just in time for Stephanie to explain that she was now intending to come over for a visit.

Richard was totally in his element at the thought of seeing his wife again, even though it was not really him she wanted to see. It was arranged between both parties that Stephanie was going to visit in the last week in January. Richard could hardly wait to see her and Jack; it had been so long, and Jack had certainly changed in the photos that they had sent. To keep his plans to himself about the idea of moving was going to prove a huge task. The excitement of wanting to be near Stephanie and learn to be loved by her again was going to be the real test of their love for one another.

If it were even possible to begin all over again, surely they would give it one hundred per cent effort and learn to love and trust once more. As the visit drew nearer, Stephanie became more hesitant over seeing Richard and eventually the reality of the fact that he wanted her back in his life. Stephanie didn't intend letting Richard back in her life at any cost, after the way she'd been treated once she'd found out about his affair with that woman!

But something seemed to stick in the back of her mind; it was niggling away at her subconscious, telling her she had to give it time to get used to the whole idea of being with the man she had meant to spend the rest of her life with!

It was only a week before Stephanie left for England, yet there was so much organising to do. She had looked at a few properties lately to consider living in with Jack, but as yet had seen none she really wanted for a home. Stephanie wanted a warm home to give her and Jack space to grow and have fun. It was harder than she actually thought it was going to be, but then she had never needed to go looking for an apartment all by herself before. But that was the way it was now, just her and Jack against the world, or that was how it seemed at that particular time, anyway!

Stephanie decided to put looking for a job on hold until her return from England. That way, she was sure of no pressures to return on the thought of going straight to work. It was definitely something she really wanted to do, and no matter how far down the ladder she might have to start, she was determined to begin a whole new life with a career to boot. The fashion business was calling out for new talent and she was sure she would manage to get a job in there somewhere.

Stephanie took Jack upstairs to think about doing some packing for the trip. Jack was a little excited about planes and so it was easy for Stephanie to slowly get him used to the idea of going on one within the next few days. The strain was eased a lot by the knowledge that his nursery hadn't been changed since they left home, so all his equipment was still there. Clothes and some of Jack's toys were really all that was needed; after all, they had left with little more than the bare essentials.

'I'm going out for a little while, Stephanie. Would you like me to pick anything up for you and Jack while I'm out?' Frances was quite at ease with the idea of the visit to England; she knew just how desperate Stephanie was to see Callum. It wasn't natural to split such a beautiful family up like they had. But it was probably Fate that dealt the cards, and not one of them could do anything about it. Frances just felt so fortunate that Stephanie had come out the coma quite quickly; that was one prayer that had been answered, thanks to Frances's faith!

'Thanks for offering, Mom, but I am going out tomorrow to get the bits I do need. We were going to have a little fun while we were out. I want to let my hair down and do something fun before we forget what the word means! Jack needs something different to keep him occupied for when we are on the plane. But thank you for offering, Mom. Have fun yourself, Mom!'

Stephanie said goodbye to her mother from the top of the stairs, and waited to hear the door close before going back into the bedroom. Stephanie managed to pack for both her and Jack by the time Frances had returned home. There was not much more that needed to be packed apart from the usual last minute stuff!

Frances had been out to visit a few close friends before she did a little light shopping. On Thursday afternoons Frances spent a couple of hours shopping with friends, eventually naming it the Thursday Club. She had had quite a few friends who'd joined her on this particular day and it kept them all close and with a lot of things to do together once a week. On one occasion Frances recalled they all had a special dinner to attend, so a group of about eight of them went out on the town and decided to buy themselves a very elegant ball gown and go in style. They had been the talk of the community for weeks afterwards!

'Let's go out for dinner tonight, Mom, what do you say?' Stephanie wanted to treat her Mom before they left New York at the weekend.

'I would love to, dear. Where would you like to go?'

There was a special little Italian place that suited families, so Stephanie booked a table for that evening, just the three of them. The conversation seemed to drown out any talk of Richard, and Stephanie was determined to discuss her future with a very reputable company she had her eye on. It meant so much for her to get back on her feet again. Stephanie had always been very organised with her life, and what direction she wanted to head in.

Jack sat in the high chair at the side of Stephanie, playing with a toy, which stuck to the tray. It seemed to keep him amused for most of the evening.

'Have you heard from Laura lately, Stephanie? I know you will be looking forward to seeing her again. I wonder if she has changed since you left?'

'Well, the last I heard, she was interested in a new fellow, but I really can't comment as I don't know if they are serious or just fooling around.'

Stephanie was happy for Laura; they meant so much to each other.

After enjoying a great meal, the three of them left the restaurant and enjoyed a stroll back to their home a few blocks away. It was only two days now until Stephanie and Jack were to leave. Frances was sure to have plenty of company with her friends, but she had come to learn to live with her daughter, after so many years away from home, that she didn't want to live on her own any more, not now. It had been awful when Harry died; she'd felt deserted and alone, and all those feelings were now beginning to creep up on her again. But these were not intended to be of knowledge to anyone else but herself! She didn't even want her daughter to know just how lonely she thought she was going to be.

It was a very pleasant evening and a lot had been discussed. Stephanie explained to Frances that her trip was only intended to last two weeks. Jack took a while adjusting to suddenly not living with his brother; as time went by, Stephanie showed Jack all the photos she could to remind him of Callum. He knew something was missing but didn't know what; Stephanie could see it in his eyes.

She was sure Callum had missed his little baby brother dreadfully, and yearned for them to be back together again. The night air began to bite a little as they all reached home. Jack began to cry a little as it was well past his bedtime and he looked so tired. 'Mom, I will just put Jack straight to bed, and I will be downstairs to sit with you in a little while, okay?'

Stephanie carried Jack upstairs and gently dressed him for bed and laid him in his crib for the night. As Frances walked through the hall, she noticed the answering machine light was on, there was a message for Stephanie from Laura.

'Stephanie, dear. There is a message from Laura on the machine for you when you come downstairs.'

Frances didn't listen to any more. She left it for Stephanie, in case there was anything wrong!

'Thanks, Mom. I'll be down in a minute.'

It had been a while since Laura had been in touch, so it was good to hear she had called, even though Stephanie had been out at the time.

Jack went to sleep really quickly and Stephanie left him to go and find out what the message said. She felt awful she hadn't been in, but that was the way things worked out sometimes. Frances stood in the dining room, reading, while Stephanie was upstairs, suddenly she could hear the excitement in her daughter's voice.

'I wish I'd been here when she rang. I hope Laura is all right!' Stephanie turned the machine on and waited for the sound of her best friend's voice.

'Hi, Steph, I am sorry I missed you. I have really missed you. I have only just found out you are coming over for a visit. I can't wait to see you. I have really missed you and I hope you are enjoying living in the Big Apple! I will catch up with you when you arrive. I'm sure Richard will be picking you up, so have a safe journey and I will see you very soon. Bye, love, Laura.'

Stephanie was even more excited now, as she was looking forward to going back now. Obviously Laura had seen Richard and he had explained what was happening, and Laura had just wanted to let her friend know how much she was looking forward to seeing Stephanie again.

'Was the news good, dear?' Frances didn't want Stephanie getting upset, so she was a little concerned.

'Laura just wanted me to know she is excited about our visit, Mom.'

Frances was just happy to hear good news and nothing upsetting.

Stephanie walked into the dining room to find her mother reading. They were quite content with each others company, and it worked quite well.

'Do you want a drink, Mom?' Stephanie sounded very tired.

'Yes, please, but then I might go to bed early, if you don't mind, Stephanie.' Frances looked almost as tired as Jack had when Stephanie had put him to bed.

They both sat at the huge dining table and talked about the evening. It had done them all good to get out for dinner for a change. Frances was going to miss them both very much while they were away.

'You will be all right, won't you, Mom, when we are away?' Stephanie always worried about her mother, even though she never let it show. Frances very rarely asked for help or anything else, for that matter.

'Of course I will be fine. Don't worry about me. I will still be here when you come back, Stephanie. You need this visit, for yours and Callum's sake. He needs his mother.'

Frances was trying to reassure herself that everything was just fine, Stephanie didn't know any different.

The day of departure finally arrived and Frances got herself worked up over Stephanie and Jack leaving. She managed to keep her composure, so as not to upset Stephanie. The only thing that kept Frances going was knowing that maybe Stephanie would return with both her sons, Jack and Callum.

Stephanie had been calm for most of the morning, but she was very excited at the prospect of seeing Callum again. Jack sat in the high chair while his mother carefully checked their luggage. Only a few last minute items needed to be thrown in for good measure. It was also double checked that Jack had his favourite toy next to him, or there would be eruptions on the journey!

'Right, then, I think we are almost ready to go to the airport, Mom!' Stephanie remarked.

'Shall I dress Jack in his coat for you, Stephanie?' Frances wanted to help as much as she could.

'Thanks, Mom.' Stephanie put her own coat on and waited for her mother to bring Jack to her.

Everyone was ready to jump into Frances's car at the front of the house. Stephanie looked back at the beautiful home and gently reminded herself she would be back soon, but for now she felt so excited.

Jack sat in his car seat, clutching his favourite teddy, not really having any idea just what was going on.

'Let's get going, shall we, Jack?' Stephanie was ready, and let her mother know as much.

The run to the airport wasn't as tedious as the departure from England. Stephanie's feelings had changed so much over the past few months. She had experienced a whole new look on life and she liked it so much. A new job was on the horizon and her plan to get Callum back looked a lot more promising than she'd first thought.

But she was in no way prepared for the announcement that Richard was going to inflict on her!

The journey was over in a short time and, before she knew it, Stephanie and Jack were boarding the plane bound for England.

As soon as their faces disappeared out of public view Frances broke her heart. She was sure that Stephanie and Jack had left for good. She watched the plane leave the runway, wishing she was flying with them, but she knew her daughter would have to do this on her own. It was Stephanie's time to be with Callum as soon as they arrived safely in England. All the way home in the car, Frances tried to think straight as the tears fell on her face. She stopped at Corrine's house and sat with her for a few hours, just for the company. The feeling of loneliness was incredible. She had never thought she would feel like that again, but she was wrong!

Corrine tried to cheer her friend up but it didn't really work. But Frances was pleased she had decided to pop in and see her anyway. They both talked for hours about absolutely anything they could think of, and they had a few laughs along the way too!

The visit had lifted her spirits by the time Frances left Corrine's home; they always enjoyed each other's company because they had so much in common. When Frances arrived back at her home, she felt very reluctant to open the front door, as she knew it was going to be just her rattling around for the next two weeks.

That night, Frances tried to keep herself very busy, so as not to let the emptiness bother her too much. She cooked herself a small meal and read a book for an hour which seemed to pass the time until she went to bed that evening, feeling a little better than she had that afternoon. The next morning she awoke, feeling really good, and she decided not to let it get her down, as she went about her day, doing exactly as she pleased.

Stephanie wouldn't have been so eager to leave if she knew just how upset her mother had been. So it was to be as normal as she could make life for herself, for the time being anyway!

Late afternoon the phone rang, it was Stephanie calling to say Richard had picked them up at the airport and they were all fine. It wasn't a long call as Stephanie was exhausted from the flight and Jack had been so good that she had barely noticed him through the flight. As long as they were safe, that was all that mattered, Frances thought. It gave her peace of mind to know that. Frances called Corrine immediately afterwards to let her know of the call from Stephanie, but a strange voice was on the other end of the line.

'Hello.' The voice didn't sound at all familiar, Frances thought!

'I'm sorry, I must have the wrong number – and I was calling a friend!' How odd, Frances thought, as she knew Corrine's number by heart.

'Were you calling Corrine?' the voice inquired.

'Yes, that's right. So I did call the right number?' Frances began to panic.

'I'm afraid to tell you that Corrine has been admitted to hospital. She fell and banged her head severely. Can I ask who is calling?' The voice suddenly sounded friendly.

'I'm a good friend of Corrine's. She hasn't got anyone else to look out for her, apart from her friends. My name is Frances Hayes and I only live a few houses away. Is there anything I can do to help?'

'If you could just lock up for her and come to the hospital to see her later. My name is Dr Sara Collins, if you need to talk to me concerning Corrine.'

'I will be there in a few minutes.' Frances put the phone down and grabbed her coat and keys and ran out of the door. It turned out that Corrine had slipped and fell within a short period of Frances leaving – which didn't make Frances feel any better. At least the doctor had been polite enough to pick the phone up and speak to her, she thought. Corrine was in the best place for the care she needed, and Frances was going to be there when she was able to see visitors.

Not that Corrine had any family, because she had never had children and very few relatives were still alive. But she had Frances and that was important, as over the years, they had both been there for one another. Frances went straight to the hospital to see her friend and give her all the support she needed. She thought she had had enough of hospitals lately, but there was nothing she could do about it. Frances was all Corrine had now. Francis couldn't think of anything more important than being there for her best friend, just as Laura had been there for Stephanie.

Corrine was put on a ward for observation that evening and watched very carefully by the nurses. Frances left the hospital after checking on her friend and went home even more tired. It had been a truly extraordinary day for her, one she probably wouldn't forget in a while. That night Frances couldn't sleep at all. As she lay awake in her bed, thinking about Harry, she suddenly didn't feel alone any more. She generally thought of Harry at night, when she was alone with her thoughts and lost in her own world. As the sun rose, Frances decided to get out of bed and watch the sunrise on her porch. The aroma of hot coffee wafted through the early morning air as Frances sat alone. She felt lucky to be alive and in good health. At least she was fit enough to look after Corrine when she came out of hospital; Frances was sure it would be better to have Corrine move in with her until she was well enough to go back to her own home.

After that, Frances knew she had to call the hospital to see how her friend was recovering. As she left the porch and went inside to make another pot of coffee she suddenly felt a cold shiver run down her spine; it almost took her breath away. The last time she had felt a sensation as strange as that was when Harry had passed away.

Oh, my dear lord, thought Frances, it couldn't be, not Corrine!

'Hello, could I possibly find out how my friend Corrine is

doing this morning? I am a close friend, Frances Hayes.' Now Frances was really concerned and very worried.

'Are you the lady who came in yesterday and stayed most of the evening?' The voice was obviously one of authority on the ward.

'Yes, I came in almost immediately from locking up her home for the doctor,' explained Frances.

'I am afraid you're friend didn't make it through the night, Mrs Hayes. I am so sorry, but she did sustain bad head injuries,' the nurse said.

'What happens now?' Frances asked in a tearful voice.

'Maybe you should come in and collect her belongings and sign a few forms, which we will explain in more detail when you arrive,' the nurse said calmly.

'All right. I will be in as soon as I can. Goodbye.' Frances put the phone down and broke down in tears. She had really thought that Corrine would be home with her in a few days. The rest of the morning was a complete blur, as Frances walked around in a daze. Dr Sara Collins was waiting on the ward when she got there. It was all so formal and clinical.

Frances was asked to sign a few forms, being the nearest to kin Corrine had now. It was so sad. Corrine had only had her friends. That was what made Frances feel so lucky, that she at least had Stephanie and her grandsons, who meant so much to her. Frances was allowed then to say goodbye to her dear friend for the last time, and returned home with only the small overnight bag that she had taken with her the previous night. All the way home, the only thought that went through her mind was that there were not many people she knew of to actually inform of any funeral arrangements.

At least she had been there for her in her hour of need. It was fate that had lead her to call Corrine that afternoon to say that Stephanie and Jack had arrived safely in England. If she hadn't done so, then she probably wouldn't have found out for a few days and by then it would have been too late to do anything for her and be there for her when she needed a friend most! All that was left now for the poor woman was to organise a dignified burial with the few friends she had left in this cruel world.

It was so difficult for Frances to concentrate, with all that had happened in such a small space of time. But Frances believed in fate and when it was your turn to leave there was absolutely nothing you could do about it. She had that belief since the day Harry had passed away, and she wasn't about to change the way she thought after all these years. Frances left it late in the afternoon before calling Stephanie to explain what had happened.

'Is that you, dear. It's only your mom. I wanted you to know my friend Corrine fell in her home and she died in hospital.'

There was an awful silence on the other end of the phone. 'Oh, Mom, I am so sorry. I know you were good friends. Do you want me to come home to be with you?' Stephanie couldn't bear to think of her mother being so distraught on her own. Surely it would be best if she were to fly back to her mom!

'No, Stephanie. I will be okay. I just wanted you to know I have a lot to do and I may not be in at times when you call. You need to be with your family right now, and my friends need to be with me. Anyway, how are things going between you two?' Frances wanted to know if her daughter was coping all right on her own over there.

'Well, things are a lot different. Richard is being very good to us. It is a little strange but we are all fine. Mom, it's great to see both my sons together again. We have missed each other so much. I will ring you in a few days when everything has calmed down for you. I love you so much, Mom. Take care of yourself.' Stephanie was upset as she said goodbye to her mother.

The conversation didn't last too long and Frances felt lonely once more. How could life be good one minute and be so cruel the next?

Corrine was a lovely lady and Frances thought a lot of her as a friend. It had all been a shock and, as Frances rang round the few remaining close friends to tell them of Corrine's death, she began to think of a few things to say about her on the day. The arrangements kept her quite busy for the next few days, until the day of the funeral arrived. It was a solemn affair and, as a few friends gathered at the local chapel, Frances tried to keep her composure while she and others paid their last respects. The funeral was a very small one but Frances thought that might be what Corrine wanted. Frances read a beautiful verse from the Bible, followed by a poem of love and friendship, which she miraculously managed to write by hand.

Afterwards, Frances invited those who kindly attended back to her home. It was a gesture she could at least offer for the flowers and kind words people had offered in Corrine's memory.

A small gathering kept Frances company for the following hours. The stories they had to share about the fun they had all shared over the years, and they shared a few laughs too. When the last of the stories had been told, and the last of the friends had left, Frances sat on her porch and hoped that she had done her friend proud with the send-off they had given her. It was the least they could do! Amazingly enough Frances wished at that particular moment if and when, she may get the same kind of love and affection from the same friends. It was a morbid yet happy thought that Frances pondered upon.

Chapter Ten

Stephanie was beginning to enjoy being back home again, but she wasn't sure just what Richard was up to! Richard was being more than nice, he was being extremely generous. It was unnerving and at times quite disturbing, as the way he had treated Stephanie before she left was unforgivable. But the devoted mother had felt it was time to fly out and see her son for the first time in months. She had considered it all carefully, yet she hadn't foreseen the actual lengths Richard would go to, to salvage his marriage. Even though the papers had been issued, it still wasn't over in his eyes!

Callum had certainly grown since she had last seen him, and Richard commented on how many new clothes he had to go out and buy for him. But Richard had become very domesticated while it was just Callum and himself. Was it at all possible that maybe, just maybe, he was a changed man?

It was indeed a very hard question she could not yet answer.

Stephanie spent every breathing moment wondering how to get back custody of Callum. 'Richard, could I talk with you sometime this afternoon?' she said rather awkwardly.

'Sure. What's on your mind, Steph?' he said casually.

'Later, Richard, when the boys have gone to bed.' She insisted the matter could wait.

Callum played with Jack all afternoon as if they had never been parted. Stephanie was wandering just how he would react when she finally came back home, but it had gone so well – better than she had hoped for. Stephanie was also hoping that when she got round to speaking to Richard that he might let her take Callum back with her!

It was a lot for her to wish for but, if she didn't ask, she knew she wouldn't get what she wanted.

As the evening drew in and bedtime was looming, Richard took the boys upstairs and bathed them before putting them to bed. But it was both of them Callum wanted to read his bedtime story. As they both sat there side by side at his bed, they looked over at each other like old times. Stephanie saw something in Richard's eyes; she wasn't sure what but something was definitely there. He kept staring at her all through the story they were reading. Stephanie had noticed this, but not so much that he would see it bothered her. Somehow she sensed that Richard was behaving like a lovesick puppy!

Just the thought of Richard getting stupid ideas into his head was annoying. She had come all the way over to England to be with the son he had taken from her, and all he could do was make eyes at her. She felt angry yet flattered that he thought he could win her back. Just how gullible was she? she thought to herself.

After they had finished the story, both her little angels were sound asleep, so they both left the room as quietly as they could, so not to disturb them. It felt strange being in the boy's bedrooms again with Richard reading to them; it was as though nothing had ever happened between them.

They walked down the stairs together and sat in the lounge to share a glass of wine. The atmosphere was beginning to get strangely romantic, but she hesitated for a moment and decided not to make an issue out of it!

Stephanie was the one who opened the conversation so she could see what they were capable of discussing. 'Richard how have you found things since I've been gone? Have you managed all right?' She wasn't sure what to expect from him.

'Well, it hasn't been easy, but when I found a crèche for Callum, things began to work themselves out after a while. I had to go to work; they weren't going to let me have much more time off and I had to go back to the office sometime – although a lot of them have no idea why I was away for so many weeks!' Richard felt he had to explain himself, as she had the right to know what was happening!

'I'm pleased for you, you seem to have everything under control. Callum seems to be very well looked after and I have just seen how he has grown.' Stephanie was anxious now to get to the point.

'You look good, Steph. How have you been coping?' he said.

'Mom has enjoyed the company and it has been good to go

back to the States. Where else would I have gone? I have begun to look for a place of my own, and maybe a job if I am lucky. Jack has missed you, and Callum, too. I could sense he knew something was missing but he is still little! They get on well, don't they, considering?' Stephanie was slowly working her way to a particular question.

'I have changed, Steph. I know I treated you really badly, and I know I owe you a huge explanation, but honestly I still have feelings for you and they will never change!' he said boldly.

'But we are officially divorced, almost, you don't seriously think that one visit is going to change all that has happened, do you?' she snapped.

'Can we start again? I want you back, Stephanie. Can't you see that I am still in love with you!'

Words were getting heated now and Stephanie could see an argument brewing. But that wasn't what she wanted. She wanted to take her son back to the States with her and bring both the boys up together. Richard was actually looking for more than just a quick visit; he had something more permanent in mind.

'I don't really know, Richard. Can I really trust you after what you did to me last year?' She was confused and anxious.

'Look, I was stupid. What more do you want from me? I don't want to lose what we once had, Steph. You loved me once, didn't you?' Richard said, looking wishful.

'There are still feelings for you, Richard, but I don't know if they are the same ones that you have. Of course I love you – you are the father of my children – but you have to understand that I have changed. I can never forgive you for what you did to me. I was in a coma because of your other woman.' Stephanie feared now to ask of his intentions concerning Callum.

'I want you to know I haven't seen her or had anything to do with her since it happened, and I know I deserved the beating that I got because of it, too. Please give me another chance, Steph. I will never let you down again, I promise,' Richard begged.

The situation was now beginning to get pretty intense in the lounge and both of them wanted to tell the other something important. Stephanie found it unbearable to see a grown man beg.

Richard and Stephanie were obviously at a crossroads of

decisions, and neither of them wanted the situation to deteriorate to breakdown level. The conversation was actually getting somewhere; they both sat down and began letting their feelings flow with confidence.

But Stephanie still hadn't fully understood just how desperate Richard was becoming. Both faces looked confused as they sat silently in the lounge thinking to themselves.

'Can we sort this mess out without any bitterness? Because I love you, but I don't think I can take you back. I am sorry, Richard, but it's too late.'

Stephanie sat back, making herself more comfortable in the chair across the room from her estranged husband.

'Is this really how you want to be? Can't you just at least give it some thought?' Richard was heartbroken and distraught at the fact that she didn't want him back. He had made the biggest mistake of his life and now he was paying dearly for it. All he could do now was try to decide if it was worth trying to get her in a different way.

An idea sprang to mind but he would have to wait until he knew for sure it would work! Richard apologised for giving her a hard time and went to bed, feeling a little more than let down.

Stephanie stayed up until the early hours to give herself breathing space and to contemplate asking Richard about her position with Callum, but she was preparing herself to get knocked back at the suggestion, considering she had knocked back his advances that evening. Stephanie remembered where they kept their family photo albums and sat for hours browsing through the memories of their life together. There had been truly happy times and a lot of fun, but they managed to misplace themselves somewhere along the way. She wondered if they could ever be that way again. Then, by chance, she pulled out a box from the same unit where all the photos were stored and she realised it was a box of things that she had treasured from the day they were married. Tears streamed down her face as she sat in a heap on the carpet, looking through their once very special day!

How odd that she hadn't thought to take it with her to the States. Even though it had all gone sour, she couldn't have wanted to lose this prized possession. In fact, Stephanie realised she never actually regretted leaving Richard: she just regretted his affair that had almost cost her her life. As tears soaked her face, a smile broke through the vision of them both standing side by side outside the church on their wedding day. The memory was still fresh in her mind, and the sweet scent of her bouquet that she had held on her most special day.

As she flipped through the pages of carefully protected photos, she sat there thinking to herself, wondering where it had all gone wrong. Why had Richard gone to someone else for what he needed, instead of her? Surely he would have understood how she felt, considering she was heavily pregnant with Jack. But she wouldn't have let him go elsewhere! The damage had been done now and if she were to let Richard back into her life, for whatever reason, then it would show she really needed him. And that she wasn't going to let happen. As the past few months had proved, she had got her life back on track and begun to pick up the pieces of her broken dream.

She had to do this on her own and prove she didn't need a man in her life, especially one like Richard Sandlers! Even though she had moved to a large city full of attractive men, Stephanie felt she didn't really need one. She was happy to be single again and it was a very content feeling. She still had feelings for Richard, but they would never be able to be the same together.

That night, Stephanie couldn't sleep at all, she had so many memories floating around in her head. She kept thinking of the photos and box of memories filled with love and laughter. It was as though her heart was telling her not to let go, but deep down she knew that it was time to start a fresh and leave her old life behind. Strange how it felt; Stephanie didn't know where to turn after that.

She was already in the dining room when Richard came downstairs.

Although she had very little sleep, she looked very beautiful standing there gazing out of the window, still dressed in her dressing gown. Ironically, it was the one he had purchased for her when she was in hospital. As she stood there with her long hair flowing over her shoulders, she was youthful as the day they met. Stephanie hadn't changed at all; if anything, she had grown even more beautiful, and Richard's heart melted as he stood there in the doorway staring at her.

He could barely stop himself from staring, and as she turned around she saw him, their eyes locked and Stephanie held him under the same spell that attracted him so many years before! As she stood there, she realised how he was staring and she moved across the room to sit down at the table. It was as if she knew he was there and watching her, but as soon as she turned around she felt awkward somehow!

'Just how long have you been standing there, Richard?' she said quietly.

'Not long. I saw you and decided to look at how beautiful you looked before you saw me. Sorry if I surprised you,' Richard mumbled to himself.

Neither of them knew what to say to each other, as the feelings they were both harbouring might upset the other. It was a truly compromising situation, but the silence was broken by the sound of little feet coming down the stairs.

Callum came into the dinning room still rubbing his weary eyes, and kindly remarked that his little brother was awake, too! 'Mummy, can I have some toast?'

Callum reacted to his mother as if she had never gone away. It felt so natural to see both his parents in the same room together, especially in the morning.

'Of course you can, sweetheart. I will go and bring Jack down and you can sit together, okay?' Stephanie gave her son a big hug and kissed him on the cheek.

Stephanie said nothing to Richard as she walked past him and her scent almost caught his breath; he had forgotten how good his wife smelled! As she went upstairs, her scent wafted through the hall like a meadow in full bloom. It was wonderful, Richard thought to himself. But how long would all this last? In less than a week Stephanie would be back on the plane, leaving the country once more.

Richard could hear Jack babbling to his mother as they joined the rest of the family in the dining room. It was as though they were playing happy families once more, but how was she going to explain that she was leaving so soon to go away again? Could she really expect Callum to understand what was happening?

The whole week was filled with activities for all of them and it seemed amazing just how they all got along. The atmosphere was enjoyable, yet neither made a move to ask questions that had been left on the boil for the past two weeks. It looked like it was going to be a last minute thing before Stephanie dropped her bomb on Richard. She was going to insist that she wanted to take Callum back with her; she also knew that his custody of him was temporary, after which she was entitled to have full custody.

Their timing was all wrong; they were having fun and it was soon to be spoiled by tears. It brought back the nightmare of her last departure, which had been a humiliating experience to say the least. One she didn't want a repeat performance of at any cost.

Stephanie's short stay soon came to a close and she began to organise herself to leave once more. It was a routine she was familiar with now and it was so easy to pack the bare essentials and travel lighter. Stephanie was in the guest bedroom, preparing Jack's little case, when Richard came in and sat on the bed to talk to her. The boys were in their bedrooms and Jack was in his playpen, quite content with his toys in there. Richard looked at Stephanie very seriously, as if he was waiting to say something to her. Of course, it was all lousy timing as it was so near to the end of her visit. Stephanie waited, hesitating as to what to expect from Richard.

'Listen, Steph, I know you won't change your mind, but I just want you to know I still love you. I don't blame you for going back to New York, but always remember I love you and I will always care for you!' Richard stood up and kissed his wife on the cheek, as he couldn't expect anything else.

At least she could still smile at him; love was still there but not quite visible to the eye.

'Look, Richard, can I talk to you?' Stephanie was puzzled over how to put the question but it had to be said.

'I thought we'd said it all, Steph. What more is there to say?' Now it was Richard who was puzzled; he had no idea what she wanted to know.

The two estranged partners sat on the bed. There was a moment of silence before Stephanie chose to say just what was on her mind. 'Richard, I have to know: will you agree to let me return to New York with Callum and Jack together? I don't think I could bear to leave him behind again. They belong together, can't you see that?' She was almost in tears at the thought of going back without Callum once more. The tension was almost crippling her.

'I have been thinking about it. Maybe if you let me keep him for a little while longer, then I will return him to your full custody after my custody period is over. Would you be satisfied with that idea?'

It was only a suggestion, but it was a start. Richard was not at all surprised at her question; he only wondered if it was the only reason for her visit.

'Well, how long were you planning on keeping him?' she asked anxiously.

'Maybe a week, two tops. I know my time is up by the end of the month anyway.' Richard was really trying to be as fair as he possibly could.

'I think we can agree on that as long as you promise to keep your word. That is one of the reasons things happened the way they did, because of the trust being mistreated!'

'Steph, I could never hurt you again. You must know that by now.' Richard made a pact with the mother of his children: right that minute, he swore on his mother's grave he would never give her any reason to hate him ever again. He had finally come to respect her once more and admire her dignity.

Now that they had come to an agreement, it was decided that Callum should know what was going on. That afternoon, both his parents sat him down quietly while Jack was asleep and explained that Daddy was to have him a little longer, then it was going to be time for him to go and live with mummy.

Callum's reaction was pretty normal. He actually liked the idea of flying in a plane to see Mummy. But not once did he question why Mummy was leaving; it was as if he had got used to both his parents living apart. Which surprised Stephanie, because he was taking the news better than she thought a child would have done! The main thing was, Callum knew exactly what was going on and he was okay with it.

The rest of the day was rather relaxing and stress-free, considering the pressure they had been under. Now that all questions were out in the open and had been answered, it was a lot calmer. They all enjoyed a relaxing day at home, playing with both of the boys.

Stephanie had yet to see her friend Laura, but because she and Richard had had a lot to sort out, she hadn't been able to see Laura yet. They had been out with the boys so much while they were together, that it seemed that Laura knew when she was intruding.

Although at that precise moment the phone rang, and it was Laura at the other end of the line. The excitement in her voice was unmistakable; like a child in a sweet shop, was the way Stephanie liked to describe her friend. After a quick chat to see if it was okay to come round and see them, Stephanie said she could hardly wait to see her. They both put the phone down and there was a knock at the door.

Stephanie didn't think any more about it, and as she opened the door a huge bouquet of flowers was thrust into her face and a bout of giggling came from behind the beautiful flowers. It was Laura; she had been at the door all along. It was a lovely greeting that Stephanie would never forget. Laura had a knack of being spontaneous and unpredictable!

'I can't believe you're back. How are you? When do you go back? Are you going back? You look fantastic: how do you do it? The States obviously agrees with you!' Laura had so much to catch up on, and in so little time to do it in.

'Well, you can talk. What has got into you? You are full of the joys of spring in the middle of January.' Both women were looking extremely well and excited at seeing one another.

'Steph, I'm getting married! Can you believe it? Me getting hitched!' Laura was ecstatic at the prospect of being a bride.

Stephanie was overwhelmed by the news and indeed very happy for her friend. It was the best news she had had in a while, besides finally getting Callum back in a few weeks time.

Both women sat in the lounge in the company of Richard and their sons. When Laura saw Jack for the first time, she squealed with delight at how handsome he was. He had changed so much since they had left, and he remembered her voice; she could still make the little guy laugh.

The hours went by, and the laughter went on for hours after the boys had gone to bed. Stephanie watched her friend describe her fiancé, the love she talked of, the things they both had in common. Laura was in awe of this man; she adored the very ground he walked on, and the feeling was mutual by the sound of it. Laura had never been as happy as she was now, and it showed tremendously. Stephanie was certainly impressed.

Laura and Stephanie only had a brief few hours left before Laura went home for the evening. They had so much fun together; they were like two little girls who had never really grown up out of their childhood giggles! Stephanie had really enjoyed the entire evening and Richard had been the perfect gentleman throughout.

It was very late when they both went to bed; even though Stephanie had to get up early, she knew it was worth it to see Laura and the news of getting married was so surprising, out of the blue like that. But Laura always liked to give a surprise now and then!

She looked in on her sons before turning in for the night. It gave her such comfort to see them so content again. They were very close and, although they had been apart for so long, it was amazing just how the bond was naturally still there!

As she tiptoed away from the door, Richard whispered, 'I love you, Steph,' and then brushed her arm gently and he touched her hand before leaving her to go into his own room, the room they used to share.

Stephanie wasn't too sure what he expected of her, but she wasn't going to respond in any other way but to go to her own room at the other end of the hall. Stephanie drifted off to sleep, thinking of a lot of things that night: the way Richard had whispered softly in her ear, and all the fun with her best friend. Her whole visit had gone rather smoothly, considering she didn't know how it was going to turn out. She accepted that it would be a week or two before she finally got custody of Callum, but that was just a formality!

Richard was due back to work again after the weekend, and it was back to New York for Stephanie, but it had all been worth it.

Laura was to be at the house the following morning to be with Stephanie for the last few hours, just as she had wanted to be there the last time she left! This time the atmosphere was much more relaxed but very emotional. They all hated long-winded goodbyes, but it couldn't be avoided at any cost. Stephanie wanted to get back to give her mother all the support she could through her friend's death. She should have gone back earlier but Frances wouldn't let her even consider it. Stephanie needed to be with her sons together as a family.

Stephanie couldn't begin to imagine what she would have done if it had been her best friend in those circumstances. It must have really shocked Frances! Although, with everything happening, it had kept Frances very busy, so she hadn't had the time to miss Stephanie that much. There was the prospect of looking for that job that she wanted so much; there was a lot to do when she returned to her mother's and eventually Callum would be joining them too, so it was even more urgent that they move into their own apartment as soon as possible!

Stephanie's plan to start a new life was beginning to look more real every time she thought about it. And, if she was perfectly honest with herself, she hadn't even considered where Richard fitted into the scheme of things. Stephanie rarely had the recurring nightmare of the accident; it was all a distant memory now, one to be forgotten. It was going to be a long healing process but one she would have to go through alone.

She no longer feared being in a car or panicking; they were long gone too! As for Richard, he would probably be plagued with guilt until the day he died over what he had done to his wife! No matter how much he told her, he knew how close he came to losing her forever.

It was early when Callum woke Stephanie; he had come into her room to see if she was still there. She gave him a huge hug and assured him that he was coming to live with her in a few short weeks. But, for the time being, she was going to be there for a few more hours yet. It was just a little reassurance that he wanted, along with a cuddle. It was a lot for a young boy to understand, but she thought that he had got the idea.

By the time Stephanie had showered and dressed, breakfast

was ready on the dining table. Richard had made an early start to the day, considering it was their last day. Stephanie dismissed his kindness and efforts as purely intentional creeping! But she wasn't falling for it; she didn't want him and that was that.

She sat down to a full English breakfast, but couldn't face eating it all. Richard was bending over backwards to please her at all times and it put her a little on edge as she wondered if it was building up to something!

Laura arrived promptly just before 8 a.m., to ensure she didn't miss any valuable time with Stephanie and Jack. She planned to go to the airport with all of them to say goodbye!

'Hi, Laura, I am glad you could make it. Did you have a good time last night? We had fun, didn't we? Just like old times!' Stephanie thought it had been a great night.

'I really miss the things like that since you've been gone, Steph! It's good we still have a laugh together.' Laura thought very highly of Stephanie; she had always been able to tell her anything, and she trusted her judgement. The reason why she hadn't brought her fiancé to meet them all was because of the recent events: that wasn't a pretty picture of married life that Laura wanted for her and her husband!

'Did I mention that we are getting married in the spring and you are all invited? If you wouldn't mind, I would like you to both be witnesses and the boys to be page boys?' Laura said with a huge smile on her face.

'I really don't know what to say. I would love to. Thank you so much!' Stephanie couldn't believe it, as Laura hadn't mentioned it the night before. They had probably drunk too much and she'd forgotten!

'Richard, you will make it, won't you?' she shouted in the dining room.

'We will be there together, whatever the circumstances, Laura. We wouldn't miss it for the world.'

Stephanie was excited for her. She had never been this in love before. Sure, she had had men in her life but none serious enough to propose! It gave Stephanie something more positive to look forward to, and help in the preparations if needed.

It was to be held in a small chapel a few miles away, but they all knew where it was: it was a beautiful little chapel, and big enough for what Laura wanted. The man Laura was planning to many was called Hayden Thomkins; he was a successful businessman who owned his own travel bureau. Laura had met him by chance and they had been attracted to one another instantly. She hadn't looked back since then.

Stephanie could only wish her all the luck in the world for a happy and blessed marriage, unlike her own. Jack would almost be one year old when Laura was to get married, she also wandered if Laura wanted children once she and Hayden were married!

Another scene at another airport was beginning to become almost routine. It was the saying goodbye that hurt so much. The feelings between Stephanie and Richard became more apparent as it came to leaving. Laura could tell there was something going on behind that dignified smile that Stephanie always showed. Was she afraid to give her heart for the sake of a stupid mistake? Laura didn't ask any questions, just thought to herself. Afraid that if she interfered in any way, it might ruin her friends' last chance of giving her marriage another chance to survive!

So, as tears were rolling down her pale pink cheeks, once more she said her goodbyes and turned her back to catch her flight back to New York. As they watched the plane leave on the runway, there were tears again. Laura commented that the next time she saw Stephanie would be very near her wedding day!

The plane took off into the sky and left Laura and Richard with Callum staring at something that was no longer there. They were gone and there wasn't anything anybody could do about it.

'Richard, do you think you two will ever get it together again?' Laura asked seriously.

'I am working on it, believe me!' His tone sounded optimistic and cheerful.

Laura didn't say any more on the journey home, but she played with Callum to keep him occupied. The ray of sunshine that had come into their lives had disappeared, leaving a feeling of sadness and loneliness behind her. Stephanie didn't belong away from her family; they shouldn't be living in separate countries, but they were.

It was all up to Richard to fight for her and make her listen to her own heart! When they arrived back at the house, Richard offered Laura a drink but she declined his offer and went about doing her own thing. She had a wedding to prepare and the day would be there before she knew it, so she left Richard's to get herself organised. As for Richard and Callum, well, they had to get on with their lives too. There was much to do if he wanted to arrange to move to the States to be with his estranged wife.

Richard hadn't told a soul about his plan in case it didn't work out. So he tried to do almost all the work and checking out things on his own, which proved to be somewhat difficult to begin with as he still had a full time job and a child to look after. The ideas were all on paper; putting it into action was the difficult part.

The rest of the weekend, Richard spent enjoying time with Callum. They went out to the park, played ball and Richard even took Callum to the zoo, but that wasn't the same without Stephanie beside him as she had been for the last two weeks! It was slowly killing him inside to be without her, but she hadn't taken any notice of his intentions to try to work it out. That was what he thought, anyway! He had seen how she was still beautiful with her slim elegant figure, the way he remembered. Stephanie was constantly on his mind day and night. He had to win her back, and he should never have lost her in the first place.

If you were lucky in this life, you were given a second chance and that was what Richard was working towards! He didn't care if he ended up permanently living in New York, as long as he could have his family back together again. He had never wanted anything more in his life than he wanted Stephanie and Jack back. As Richard looked at Callum, he wondered what Stephanie would be thinking right that very same moment. Could it be possible that she was thinking along the same lines as he was? Only time would tell, now; no one else could make it happen.

Goodbyes were always one thing that Stephanie hated about leaving those she loved behind. There were always tears and pressure to stay but she had to go; there was a new life waiting to be explored.

On the other side of the world it was pretty much the same story. Stephanie was almost near the end of her journey and as she looked out of the plane window she felt empty. The kind of feeling you have when something is missing and you don't know how to replace it. She knew what it was, it was Richard that was missing, but it was too late now. She felt exhausted but she wasn't able to rest properly, unlike Jack. Jack was a brilliant baby; he could go to sleep anywhere at all!

As the plane landed on American soil, Stephanie couldn't get Richard off her mind. The flight was over and she was back home again. Stephanie had come to consider this her home now, no matter what happened.

Stephanie had contacted her mother a few days beforehand, and let her know what the flight times were. Frances had said she would be there to pick them up. They were both looking forward to seeing each other again. Frances had been through so much during the last two weeks. She was definitely looking forward to seeing them and hearing all about their trip. When they finally found each other it was really emotional. As mother and daughter hugged each other they began to cry. 'I have only been gone a couple of weeks, Mom,' Stephanie said, feeling overwhelmed.

'I know, but it's good to see you.' Frances was so choked up she could hardly speak.

As they chatted away while Stephanie waited for her luggage, Frances was saying how well they both looked and she had already noticed a difference in Jack. Maybe he had grown, or he just looked fuller in the face; she wasn't quite sure. Frances was more relaxed to have them home again; she had missed them so much and she told Stephanie as much. It had been busy, but she had felt so lonely, especially when Corrine passed away so suddenly.

Jack was placed in his car seat, as always, in the front of the car and he loved that. He could see everything from that seat. All the way home Frances spoke of what had happened in more detail, and there was hardly a chance for Stephanie to say anything until they were practically on the doorstep!

Stephanie realised it was probably because Frances had had no one else to confide in at the time; she hadn't wanted Stephanie to cut her trip short, so she had put up with the whole situation on her own, only now she was letting it all out. The loneliness, the loss of a friend, and being on her own and also the flood of memories of losing Harry! It had all been too much for her to cope with on her own, really. But Stephanie was back and Frances could tell her anything she wanted to.

'Mom, I'm so sorry about Corrine. I know she was a really old and good friend to you.' Stephanie wasn't quite sure what to say, but she let her mother know she was there for her.

It was a time to reflect on her feelings. Stephanie couldn't bear to think what she would do if that had happened to her friend Laura. From that moment, she almost understood just what her mother had been going through alone. But her mother looked well; at least she had been taking care of herself. Jack had been the perfect companion; Stephanie told her how good he had been on both flights. He had been no trouble at all; he had the flight attendants spoiling him. As she took him out of the car and gave him to Frances, he let out a giggle and laughed at her!

'Yes, I've missed you, too,' she said, tickling him.

'If you take him inside, Mom, I will bring the cases in.' Stephanie took time to look around her before she went inside. She loved this part of town; it was pleasant and quiet. She wanted most of all to raise her sons here, where she had found happiness.

Richard's name wasn't even mentioned by Frances as she didn't quite know how things went!

Frances could see there was something bothering her daughter. She could see it in her eyes; there was definitely some kind of sparkle. Yet Stephanie had no idea those around her had seen it, too.

'You still love the man, don't you, Stephanie?' her mother suggested.

'I honestly do not know right now, Mom!' Stephanie said, trying to avoid the subject.

They all sat down for dinner that evening and talked about everything, what had been said by Richard and the way he felt about her. Stephanie explained how she had rejected his advances to make up, and how he was bending over backwards to get her back!

As Frances looked into her daughter's eyes, she began to believe that Stephanie was afraid to trust him again. He had changed but Stephanie hadn't given him a chance to see just how much she could trust him. The other woman involved had not been mentioned since. So it was safe to assume that he had finished with her most definitely.

Stephanie bathed Jack that night and put him to his bed utterly exhausted from travelling. And she then continued to talk to her mother well into the small hours of the morning. They had discussed issues that they had never spoken about before and it was fantastic, the topics that they were able to talk about.

It also made Frances feel a whole lot better to know that they were home safe meant a lot too. Although she wasn't sure about the idea of Richard keeping Callum for the extra weeks: she thought he might be up to something. But Stephanie put her straight on that one.

'It will be okay, I trust him!' She knew what it was as soon as she saw her mother's face!

'Do you realise what you said?' Frances asked, sounding more shocked.

'Yes, I do.' Stephanie was surprised herself; she stood for ages with her hand over her mouth in a state of shock. She knew what it meant: she trusted her husband enough to know he wasn't going to cheat on her again. All she had to do was believe what she already knew – she still loved him!

Stephanie had to sit down to calm herself a little. She felt like a lovesick teenager again. She kept saying over and over in her mind that she did love him, after all. She had never stopped; she had just hidden it out of the way so she wouldn't get hurt again.

They both went to their beds that night shattered and confused with all that had happened. Again Stephanie had a sleepless night, thinking what it would have been like if she had realised how she felt sooner. She felt happy, but also terrified. She wasn't sure how things would change, now she knew the truth!

Things were beginning to feel normal again, and a week had passed since Stephanie came back from England. Stephanie needed to think about what she wanted to do, so she persuaded her mother to keep it to herself until she wanted Richard to know just how she felt. Frances agreed, but only if she made her mind up quickly, before it all went badly wrong. Stephanie seemed much happier in herself and also wasn't so tense about the situation.

Stephanie and her mother were sitting on the porch as they did on occasions. Jack was happy watching a cat on the lawn grooming itself. It was a quiet afternoon and there was nothing happening, when a yellow cab pulled up at the front of the house. Nether of them took much notice, to begin with, until the door of the cab swung open and Richard and Callum got out.

Stephanie's jaw dropped with shock. Her husband was there right in front of her with her son. As he paid the driver and walked up the little path, both his heart and hers began to beat faster and faster; their eyes met and locked. They couldn't take their eyes off each other, it was an amazing sight to see!

As for Frances, she screamed with delight to see Callum again; she held her arms out as he ran towards her.

'Hi, Steph. I just wanted to tell you again how much I love you!' He looked so handsome, yet so different. His voice was soft and warm.

'Richard, I– I love you, too. I think I always have.' Stephanie played it calm and cool as he did. It was all so spontaneous and romantic.

It was like something out of the movies, Stephanie thought. They were right for each other and always had been. The chemistry was there all along; it had never gone anywhere else. What they both finally discovered was that they had been given a second chance at love and they snatched it.

The moment was incredible and so was the timing. Both of them had been thinking so differently. Richard had been declaring his love all along while Stephanie had been in denial.

The reunion lasted for hours with tears and laughter. The boys were delighted at being together again and played while their parents enjoyed the celebrations. Frances was thrilled at the whole idea; she had known there was something different when Stephanie returned from her visit.

At last the family were together for the first time since Stephanie was in hospital. They had all truly come a long way since that awful experience. Richard's prayer had been answered and he was overwhelmed that his wife had never stopped loving him!

'When did you decide to fly out here, Richard?' Stephanie was curious.

'I have been planning to for weeks now, love.' Richard gazed into her eyes and kissed her so gently it made her lips tingle!

'Let's sell up in England and start afresh out here. What do you say, Steph?' he said, staring at her beautiful face.

'I think I agree with you, I love you, Richard Sandlers.'

She was every bit in love with him as he was with her, all they had needed was a break from each other, not a divorce!

Spring arrived and in England the flowers had just come into bloom. It was a beautiful Saturday afternoon, and as the vintage bridal car arrived everyone took their seats in the chapel. The organist began to play the Wedding March as Laura entered the chapel dressed in the most amazing bridal gown anyone could wish to wear. She was the most beautiful bride Stephanie had ever seen. As Richard and Stephanie stood behind the bride and groom, they looked into each other's eyes and whispered the marriage vows to each other. And as the celebrations began and the confetti was thrown, it was two marriages that had been blessed that day, not just one!

Printed in the United Kingdom
by Lightning Source UK Ltd.
1200